# DEADLY
# REFLECTIONS

## Terri O'Brien

PublishAmerica
Baltimore

ISBN: 1-4241-8304-9
PUBLISHED BY PUBLISHAMERICA, LLLP
www.publishamerica.com
Baltimore

Printed in the United States of America

This book is dedicated to my husband, Pat, whose wonderful love and constant encouragement, gave me the courage to see my book make it to print, and fulfill that dream. Thank you for teaching me to trust in my heart.

# Acknowledgment

Thank you to my very special parents, Ray and Marge, whose unconditional love always lets me know how proud they are of me, and for that I will always be grateful.

# Chapter One

*December 2005—Denver, Colorado*

If he were just dead, life would be so much easier. The thought raced through Emma Hudson's mind, as she angrily kicked off her Gucci leather boots, leaving them in a pile of snow and slush by the front door. Strands of colorful Christmas lights reflected off the deep mahogany walls, adding warmth to the foyer, while lighted candles filled the air with the festive scent of Bayberry. It was supposed to be the season of love and joy, but, all Emma felt tonight was pain and misery. As much as she hated to admit it, she was more angry with herself, than with her husband. Once again, she had allowed him to berate her in public without so much as a word in her own defense. Shrugging off her charcoal wool coat, she shook the last of the snow off, and tossed it over the banister, not caring that it left small puddles of water on the Italian marble floor.

The quietness of the stately Tudor house was nothing unusual. Its rooms had never been filled with laughter, or family gatherings, only the stuffy dinner parties given for Charles' more wealthier clientele. Tonight, however, there was a strangeness to the quiet that left a knot in the pit of Emma's stomach. Maybe she was just hungry. After all, she hadn't bothered to eat any dinner after Charles stormed out of the fund raiser. Walking through the dark dining room towards the kitchen, Emma stumbled over one of Otis' toys, catching herself on the sideboard. As she moved the toy aside with her foot, she suddenly felt very lonely.

"Oh, Otis, I wish you were home. Why did I let you spend the night at Grandma's."

Emma would love to have had someone to talk to right now. It was too late to call her mother, and Allison probably wasn't home yet. Allison, her best friend, and Charles' legal assistant, had only witnessed the tail-end of Charles' tirade. Emma decided that tomorrow she would drag Allison out to lunch, and fill her in on what happened.

The overhead lights in the kitchen gleamed off the stainless steel appliances as Emma entered through a large, swinging door. Taking inventory of the refrigerator's contents, she opted for a sandwich made out of the left over ham. Emma pulled a small butcher knife from the cutlery block on the counter next to the refrigerator, and sliced several thick pieces of ham off the bone. After laying the dirty utensils in the sink, she poured herself a glass of milk, picked up the plate, and headed for the library.

This was Emma's favorite room in the entire house because it was all her's. She had decorated it without one ounce of input from Charles. The bookshelves contained everything from signed, first edition prints to paperbacks that could be purchased at any discount store. Curling up in one of the big, overstuffed chairs, Emma picked up the current novel she was reading, and opened it to where the worn leather bookmark stuck out of the top. She munched on her sandwich and tried to concentrate on the words before her, to no avail. The evening had been long and stressful, and Emma just wanted to fall into her soft, warm bed. She decided to take the rest of the milk with her upstairs, and placed her empty plate on the small table in the front hall. Noticing one of the lines on the phone was lit up, Emma closed her eyes and let out a pent-up sigh. So, Charles was home after all. Emma had been sure once he left the party, that he was going to spend another night at the "office".

Reaching the top of the stairs, she observed the dim light that was coming from under their bedroom door at the end of the hall. Emma traced the intricate pattern in the dark Persian rug covering the hall floor with her big toe for several minutes, while she studied her options. The guest bedrooms at the opposite end of the house beckoned to her, but she knew things would only get worse if Charles found out she was home, and didn't tell him. To steady her nerves, Emma took a deep breath, then opened the door.

The enormous master bedroom consisted of two separate rooms. All of the furniture was dark mahogany, and very masculine in appearance. Emma had never felt comfortable here. The long, dark blue, velvet drapes gave the room a somber feel. Even the light from the fire in the massive, marble fireplace couldn't penetrate the wavering shadows around the room. A loud, popping noise from behind startled her, and Emma whipped her head around. A glowing ember flew out from the opening in the fireplace, as the pine sap in the logs heated and expanded until it released that energy in a tiny explosion. Several other embers were already dying on the expensive Persian rug in front of the hearth. Something was wrong. Charles would have never left the protective screen from in front of the fireplace. Emma scooted the brass screen back into place, and walked towards the adjoining bedroom, which was just as dark as the outer sitting room. A small lamp on the bedside table was the only light in the room. From somewhere in the background, the repeating sound of a busy signal reached her ears. Charles' tuxedo jacket, designer shirt, shoes and socks were strewn across the floor. Emma could see him lying face down on the bed.

"Charles?" Emma said in a half whisper. Receiving no answer, she tried again, a little louder this time. "Charles? I wanted to let you know I'm home." There was still no movement from the bed. She knew that he had had a number of drinks tonight, but, hadn't thought it had been enough to cause him to pass out.

As she approached the bed, Emma could see the dark, crimson stain that was weaving its way into the creme colored, satin sheets and pillows. An acrid, coppery smell assaulted her nose, and her stomach started to churn. Edging forward, she felt a warm, sticky substance on the bottom of her foot. Sure that it must be blood she stepped in, Emma looked down and saw the tip of a blade that belonged to a large butcher knife peeking out from under her toes. Her mind flashed to the cutlery block downstairs in the kitchen, where one of the slots had been empty.

Panic started to set in, and Emma's first impulse was to run. But, if there was chance that Charles was still alive, she had to try to help him. Reaching towards his body, her hand stopped midway when she thought she heard a soft, rustling sound. Emma remained still for several minutes, searching the shadows for the source. She heard nothing more, and turned back to the gruesome scene before her. Charles' skin felt cool to her hand, as she grabbed his shoulder and rolled him over. The mutilated condition of the body was more than Emma had bargained for. She wasn't sure whether the screams she heard were real, or in her head, but, as her knees buckled under her, Emma had the distinct feeling she was being watched.


*Three Months Later*

The last of the moving boxes had been placed in the back of the rental truck parked in Emma's circle drive. After several tugs on the burlap strap, the stuck, overhead door finally slammed shut, echoing in the half-empty truck. A Realtor® sign, with "Sold" pasted across the front, swung back and forth in the warm, Chinook wind blowing off the Rockies. The house had sold quickly, within days of going on the market. Its location in the prestigious Cherry Creek neighborhood of Denver had been the main reason, but the recent murder had also attracted a number of offers from some rather strange people. Her real estate agent had helped Emma sort through the contracts, and they had settled on an offer that included all the furnishings in the house. The only things packed in the moving truck were items of a personal nature. Emma stepped back and surveyed the small mansion before her.

The grey stones and mortar were cold and uninviting, eliciting very little in the way of anything memorable from her. There was little Emma was going to miss from the last two years of her life, except for Allison and David. She worked with them at the law firm, and they had been there whenever she needed them over these last few months. Goodbyes had been said last night over a quiet, dinner at their favorite Italian restaurant downtown on Larimer Square. Allison and David had tried, one last time, to convince Emma not to move, but she knew she was doing the right thing.

Lieutenant Roger Harris turned his tan Ford Taurus into the driveway of the Hudson estate. He was the lead investigator on the murder case, and had come to give Emma an update. His superiors had informed him yesterday that the investigation was to be closed, and listed as a fouled burglary attempt. Harris knew that someone must be putting pressure on the District Attorney's office, but, when he asked questions, he had been shut out. Having to tell Emma was the part of his job that Harris hated. Emma seemed oblivious to him, as he pulled in behind the rental truck.

"A penny for your thoughts," Harris said, as he got out of the car.

Emma gave him a small smile. "That's about all their worth right now."

"An intelligent woman like you? I'm sure their worth a lot more than that." Harris reassured her with a little wink. Emma truly liked the balding detective, who treated her with both respect and kindness. "Looks like you're all packed."

"Yeah. I was just taking one last look around." They stood in silence for a moment, then she reached over and hugged him. "Thank you for all you've done."

Her unexpected display of affection made him feel self-conscious. "You're welcome, Emma."

"Well, I'd better get going. Otis is already waiting in the truck."

"I'm going to miss you both." Harris had been stalling, but now he had to tell her. "Before you go, Emma, I need to fill you in on the most recent development on the case."

"What kind of development?"

"They're halting the investigation."

"What?!"

"It seems the higher ups have concluded that Charles' murder was the result of a burglary gone bad. Just being at the wrong place, at the wrong time."

"That's a bunch of crap, and you know it." Emma's voice was tight with anger. Although she found it difficult to miss Charles, even he deserved to have the authorities find out what really happened that night.

"I know, Emma, but unfortunately my hands are tied."

She ran her hands through her chestnut curls. "So, what am I supposed to do now that Charles' murderer is going to be running around loose?"

"Do you have someone you can stay with for a while? Or, I can help you hire a bodyguard."

"No! No bodyguard. I just got out of one prison." Harris had no question as to what she was eluding to.

"Listen. There's no statute of limitations on murder, and I plan to spend my spare time working this case. I want this guy caught, too." Emma could hear the conviction in his voice, and it gave her some comfort. "I'll keep you informed, and contact you when I find out anything new."

Emma nodded. "I'll call you with my new phone number as soon as I get it."

"New phone number? I thought they let you keep your number when you moved."

"Not when you're moving to Missouri."

"Missouri?" The startled look on the detective's face made her giggle. "Why Missouri?"

"I visited there several times with my folks, and it seemed so laid back. Thought it would be a nice change."

This turn of event made Harris uncomfortable, but he doubted he could change her mind. "Emma, promise me that when you get there, you'll let the local authorities know what happened here."

"Why?"

"Just to make this old man feel better, okay?"

"Okay," she smiled warmly. "But, I don't know what old man you're talking about."

Harris laughed, as he walked her to the driver's door. "You and Otis take care of yourselves."

Emma hugged him once more. "We will," she said, climbing into the cab next to Otis, who had fallen asleep on the seat.

Starting up the truck, she headed down the driveway and out onto the street, on her way to a new life. Harris pulled out behind her, turning in the opposite direction when they hit the four-way stop at the corner. Neither one of them ever noticed the plain, white car that had been parked on the street all morning long, or the stranger whose eyes burned with an evil waiting to be unleashed.

# Chapter Two

*October 2006—Cedar Falls, Missouri*

The orange autumn moon outlined the small, two room cabin that was perched on one of the many balds in the Ozark hills. Inside, the old woman sat in front of a fireplace made out of large river rock, and tried to absorb its warmth. The nights were getting colder, and the cabin's only sources of heat were either the fireplace, or the black, cast iron cookstove. Martha Quinn had never felt the need before to modernize her home, but, as she grew older, the aching in her bones sometimes made her regret that she had been so stubborn. Although the pain in her joints had a tendency to make sleeping uncomfortable, that's not what had been keeping her awake for several nights now. Since childhood, Martha knew she had a sixth sense, especially when it came to the wild things in the forest around her. However, never before had she felt such a dark force invade both her waking and sleeping hours, like she was experiencing now. Odd visions filled with random images of bodies, blood, and ghosts, plagued her, each one ending with a pair of horrible, red eyes that could have belonged to the devil himself.

There was no doubt something evil had recently come to the town of Cedar Falls, and was lingering in her beloved hills. Martha had yet to pinpoint what it was the evil was seeking, but knew that the consequences were going to be devastating. If her visions would just relinquish more details, she could go and speak to Matt Green, a deputy with the Sheriff's Department. Most of the law enforcement officials were skeptical of her, and Martha knew that many in town laughed at her behind her back, but Matt wasn't one of them. Though he gave no outward signs that he actually believed in her powers, he was never condescending when he listened to her. When the time came, she hoped that he would be open minded enough to take seriously what she told him.

A soft, scratching sound at the cabin's door made Martha reluctantly leave the warmth of the fire. Cold air flooded the tiny room as she opened the door, and a small, furry body brush against her leg as it passed by on the way to the fireplace. Shaking her head and smiling, Martha closed the door. A small, red fox was curled up on the hand woven rug, watching Martha with bright eyes, while he waited for her to return. Once she settled into her chair, Martha turned her attention to her guest.

"So, what have you found out for me?"

\* \* \*

The eyes took in everything as they strolled around the Cedar Falls town square. They were the only ones out on the street at this time of night, as the small town rolled up its streets by ten o'clock. For several nights now they had been scouting out the town, trying to determine whether not to put their plan into action. Up until today, the conflict had been pulling them in the direction of leaving, but, the unexpected arrival of someone who might know their secret, changed their mind. Tonight's foray was no longer just a reconnaissance operation. Tonight would be the start of a plan filled with death and destruction.

# Chapter Three

She could feel him again. Emma knew that he was out there, watching. Otis knew it too, since he had been sitting on the couch staring out the front window for the last half hour. Turning his head, he looked at her with uncanny, blue eyes that seemed to see into her very soul. He left no doubt that he wanted her to come and gaze out the window with him.

Emma shook her head, "Not right now, Oats, I've got work to do." She had spent the morning engrossed in the transcription of some legal tapes, in order to avoid the inevitable. The elusive apparition had made a daily appearance for about two weeks now, and Emma wondered if she was going crazy.

Otis walked over and laid his sleek, black head in her lap. He looked up at Emma, and gave a little cuff, as if to reassure her everything was okay. Tugging at the sleeve of her sweater, he managed to coaxed her to the couch. Jumping up, he lay his head on the back of the couch, once again staring out at the woods. Emma sat down beside him, her back to the window. The hairs on her neck tingled with electricity. Otis turned and cocked his head at her. The unusual color of his eyes never failed to make an impact on Emma. Anyone who had ever seen new born puppies would know that it was not unusual for them to be born with bluish eyes, yet Otis' had never changed. Now, whenever he looked at her with eyes that had become a deep, sapphire blue, appearing to be almost black sometimes, she was sure he sensed things that she could never comprehend.

That seemed even more evident today, as Otis had immediately been aware of the stranger out in the woods. Emma could no longer resist the pull of some unseen force, and turned her head towards the window. Even though it was midmorning, the fog still hung like a silver curtain in the Ozark mountains. She loved how the misty fingers weaved their way through the branches of the tall oak, hickory, and cedar trees that graced the hills around her. At first, Emma avoided looking at the opening in the trees where a narrow, dirt path led down to the creek. Instead, her gaze wandered over to the two grey squirrels playing in the hayloft of the old, red barn, which was badly in need of a good coat of paint. Tucked in beside the barn was a small garden that had turned into a breakfast buffet for a plump, brown rabbit who had decided to help himself to her veggies. The extra time spent on studying the woodland creatures was doing nothing to help curb the anxiety she felt, so, taking a deep breath, Emma let her gaze come to rest on the pathway, and there he stood.

As always, he seemed to come and go with the fog, which made it difficult for Emma to make out any kind of distinct features. From what she could see though, he appeared to be around six feet tall, with an average build, and dark hair. Emma watched him turn the collar of his jean jacket up as a barrier to the cool autumn air, and then casually lean against one of the old hickory trees. A smart woman, Emma thought, should be terrified by his presence, and her especially so, since her husband was brutally murder not that long ago. She had moved to Cedar Falls eight months ago hoping to find the security and comfort a small town might offer. The five acres on which the old farmhouse she bought sat, served not only as a secluded retreat, but as a place that she hoped to put down roots. For months, Emma had felt secure here, and she now questioned herself as to why this stranger's presence didn't concern her more than it did. As she observed him now, he never appeared to move, and she wondered, once again, if he was even real. However, Emma knew the unsettling feeling she had of being watched was not her imagination.

A voice coming out of her computer declaring "You have mail," broke her concentration. Giving the computer screen a quick glance, Emma found by the time her focus returned to the window, he was gone. She turned her attention to Otis, whose nose was still pressed up against the window pane.

"Do you know where he goes?" she asked. The dog turned his head, leaving smudged nose prints on the glass, and met her gaze.

"I think you know more than you're telling me. I never see him disappear. Come to think of it, I never see him appear, either." Otis gave her a little doggy kiss, and promptly got off the couch, heading towards the kitchen. She heard the soft squeak of the back screen door as Otis pushed it open with his nose and went outside. Shaking her head, Emma walked back over to her computer to check her mail.

The e-mail was from Allison, and Emma really wasn't in the mood to read it. She had avoided keeping in touch because it seemed to make the memories more painful. Allison tried to keep her e-mails and letters on the light side, but, Emma could read between the lines as to how worried her friend was about the move Emma had made to Missouri. Recently, it seemed that most of their correspondence consisted of Emma trying to reassure Allison that she had done the right thing. With some reluctance, Emma went ahead and clicked on the message.

*Dear Emma,*

    *Just wanted to send you a note to let you know that I will be gone for a little while. Taking a well-deserved vacation. Thought you would want to know that David has left the firm. He's been so upset since Charles' death, I could hardly get him to speak with me. I'm worried about him. I'll write you when I get back. Take care of yourself.*

*Love, Allison*

    Feeling a little guilty, Emma couldn't help enjoying the sense of relief that she would have a break from Allison's mothering. Skimming the e-mail again, she was sorry to hear that David had quit. David Meyers had been a promising, young attorney in her husband's law firm, and had everything needed to make a great lawyer. He was intelligent and resourceful, as well as good looking and likeable—the last two traits never hurt with the jury. Emma had always been touched by David's caring and compassion for his clients, whether they were one of the highest paying in the office, or an indigent case he took through the Public Defender's office. What Emma admired most, though, was David's ethics and morals, two areas her own husband didn't even seem to know existed. Nonetheless, David had idolized Charles, and had also had a small crush on Emma herself. Always the proper gentleman, David had never acted on any of his feelings towards her, but, Emma knew when he looked at her how strongly he felt. She might have even fallen for David, if she and Charles had not already been married.

    Emma had met Charles after being hired by the firm as Aaron Bellecek's legal assistant. Allison, who was working for Charles, as the firm's senior legal assistant, had introduced them. From day one, Allison had helped her navigate the shark infested waters of the big law firm, making sure Emma got off on the right foot. Allison's position also included supervisory duties, however, she never thought of herself as better than any of the other support staff, something Emma admired in her. But, what Emma came to admire most, was Allison's devotion to her young daughter. Although they were required, at times, to work late into the night, it was obvious to anyone who knew her that Allison's number one priority was her child. Being a single mother was hard, however, Allison had a way of juggling everything so that she always managed to come out on top. Being somewhat prone herself to procrastination, this was a trait Emma truly envied.

As their friendship grew closer, Emma had found herself confiding more and more in Allison, about her marriage to Charles. When they had first started dating, Charles lavished her with gifts, romantic dinners, and secret weekend getaways. All the things every woman dreams and fantasizes about. Once they were married, however, it didn't take long for her to discover it was all a facade, and that Charles intended to run their private life just like he did his business. Emma had always known Charles was a tough attorney, playing every angle, and bending the rules, almost to the point of illegalities. Treating her more like one of his clients, he dictated her every move, thought, and spoken word. Too late, Emma realized all he wanted was the perfect, robot wife, one that would never embarrass him, and the charade of a happy, stable marriage, in hopes it would help him win the race for mayor, a position he so coveted.

During their entire marriage, Emma had never quit wondering why Charles wanted to marry her in the first place. Though she was attractive, slim and petite, with beautiful chestnut-colored hair, and striking green eyes, she knew she wasn't truly what he wanted. He made no secret that he preferred the Sharon Stone type, a fact that became apparent when he would blatantly flirt with such women right in front of her without a second thought. A few months into the marriage, Emma began figure out that he had picked her only because of what he thought was her connections in the political arena. Colorado Senator John Hammond's personal secretary had been Emma's mother. Charles had been sure, by marrying Emma, he would have the Senator's backing for his campaign. Being the arrogant person that he was, it never occurred to Charles that Emma's mother's dislike, and distrust, of him would have any influence on the Senator, but, it did. Halfway through his campaign, he realized the Senator had no intention of helping to throw any political support his way. Charles lost the race by a landslide, something he would always blame Emma for. After that, their marriage turned icy and, even though she had no proof, Emma knew he was having an affair. Not having the self-confidence to file for divorce herself, Emma prayed every night that Charles would leave her, knowing full well he never would. In his mind, a divorce would not only have tarnished his reputation, but would have been seen as a personal failure, and failure was something Charles couldn't tolerate. However, none of that made much difference now, Charles was dead. Just as Emma started to type a response to Allison's e-mail, the front doorbell rang.

# Chapter Four

Jake McLean had been watching her for a couple of months now. Hired over the Internet by an anonymous client who indicated Emma was in considerable danger, all of the communications between them so far had been by e-mail. It wasn't unusual for Jake to take a case from a client he hadn't met face-to-face, but his normal practice was to require certain basic information up front, such as name, address, and phone, which he would then verify prior to beginning any work. However, this particular client had been unwilling to supply him with such information. They had also remained quite vague when he asked them to be more specific about the danger Emma was in. Their only response was they feared someone might be following her since the death of her husband.

Jake suspected his client knew more than they were telling him, but, for now, they were standing firm in only providing him with what they wanted him to know. He had remained skeptical about taking the job, even when the client had been willing to pay a fee of $500.00 per day plus expenses, no matter how long the case lasted. With his bank account nearly empty, Jake made a call to his inside source with the Denver Police Department, and obtained a copy of the file containing the investigation into the Hudson murder. The paperwork revealed Emma had been the wife of a prominent attorney, and candidate in the mayoral race, who had been brutally slain in his very expensive Cherry Creek home. The police had determined the murder was the unfortunate result of a burglary attempt gone sour. If this was true, Jake was curious as to why his client felt Emma needed protection. Upon reviewing the various documents in the file, he discovered not only had nothing been disturbed in the home, but nothing had been stolen either. Why the police closed the case he wasn't sure, but, something in his gut told him his client was right, Emma was in danger.

If he hadn't been desperate for money, Jake might have still refused to take the case. He wasn't sure he wanted that kind of responsibility again. The last time someone's life had been in his hands, Jake had failed them. Working as a United States Marshal, his last assignment had been assigned to protect a witness, Laura Campbell, who was to testify in a drug/murder trial. She was the girlfriend of one of the top cocaine dealers in the Western region, but, had wanted out and was willing to testify. His duty had been to protect her around the clock until the day of the trial. The government had put them up in a "safe house" outside of Denver, in the mountain town of Evergreen. For several weeks, things had gone along without a hitch. The trial was to start right after the holidays, and, so far, there had been no attempts on Laura's life. During their time together, Jake became impressed with how hard Laura was working to make a clean start for her and her baby daughter, Allie.

One night, shortly before Christmas, Allie became sick, running a high fever. The baby's pediatrician called in a prescription to a pharmacy not far from the safe house. Jake knew he and Laura couldn't take the baby out in the bitter, cold air, but, was hesitant to leave the two of them alone. Laura finally convinced him she and Allie would be okay, and that it wouldn't take him more than a half hour to go to the pharmacy and back. With an uncomfortable feeling in the pit of his stomach, Jake reluctantly left. Laura had been right, it had only taken him about twenty minutes, but that's all they needed.

The minute Jake stepped in the front door his instincts told him something was very wrong. The house was dark except for the colorful, old-fashioned Christmas bulbs that decorated the fireplace mantel, and the big tree in the living room. The baby's shrill cries from the back bedroom reached his ears, and he called out for Laura, receiving no answer. A cold chill surrounded him, sending a shiver up his back. Jake remained still while his eyes adjusted to what little light there was. Pulling a 9mm semiautomatic pistol from under his coat, he proceeded with caution down the hall toward the back of the house. A bright light seeped out from under the bedroom door belonging to Laura and the baby. With his concentration focused down the hall, Jake was a split second too late in noticing the figure that came out of the shadows as he passed by the kitchen. From the corner of his eye, he saw something in the figure's raised hand, right before it came crashing down upon his head. The shattering of glass rang in his ears, and warm liquid flowed down the side of his head and neck. Falling to the floor, the strong smell of wine assaulted his nose, as he slid into unconsciousness.

The stinging blast of Arctic air brought Jake back around. The door to the kitchen was standing wide open, and a cold, winter wind blew small swirls of snow into the house. A light dusting of white powder was settling on the table, chairs, and counter tops. Jake managed to sit up, leaning his back against the door frame. His head hurt like hell, and there was a sharp pain in his left cheek. Gingerly touching his face, Jake winced when he felt the gash under his eye where the bottle had cut him. The side of his face was caked with blood, and his eye was beginning to swell shut. Waves of dizziness and nausea overtook him as he tried to stand up. He was thinking of sitting back down again, when Allie's cries penetrated the fog in his brain. Scanning the floor around him, Jake tried to locate his gun, but it was gone. Picking up the dagger-like letter opener off the table in the hall, he moved toward the bedroom. The door was slightly ajar, and the baby's wails continued to ring in his ears. Something told him he was already too late to save Laura. Still, Jake stood off to one side of the door as he pushed it open, half-expecting a spray bullets to come blazing out of the room,

What lay before him made Jake's stomach roll. Laura was sprawled out on the floor by the baby's crib. She had been shot in the head at close range with the shotgun he had left with her for protection, making Laura's face almost unrecognizable. The baby lay screaming in her crib, which was splattered with her mother's blood. Stepping over Laura's body to pick up the baby, Jake noticed both of Laura's hands had been cut off at the wrist. He grabbed Allie from the crib, and cradled her in his arms, trying in vain to comfort her. Jake ignored the phone on the bedside table, and quickly left the room, telling himself it was the baby that needed to get away from the bloody scene. Once he was back in the living room, Jake rocked Allie until she fell asleep in his arms. He designed a make shift crib on the couch using every spare pillow he could find, and gently laid the baby down being careful not to wake her. Only then did Jake pick up the phone and call his office, knowing full well what the consequences of the night would mean. With their star witness dead, Laura's boyfriend, Doug Sanders, wound up with only a five year sentence for possession of narcotics. No one else had been willing to testify about Sanders' distribution network. Though an internal investigation had cleared Jake of wrong doing, Laura's murder continued to eat at him day and night, until six months later he resigned.

During the next year, Jake became a recluse, battling bouts of drinking and depression. Not working, he tried to live off what savings he had, which dwindled away faster than he anticipated. Jake's wake-up call came when he arrived home one night to find an eviction notice tacked to his front door. Taking a good, long look at himself in the mirror, and not liking what he saw, Jake made a vow to himself to become the man he once was. Opening his own private investigation firm, Jake thought it was rather ironic when most of his work wound up coming from the local criminal defense attorneys. He also did a smattering of domestic surveillance and process serving when cash got really tight. Requests had come in for what some would call more exciting and well paying jobs, such as bodyguard and undercover work, but Jake had turned them all down, until now. Try as he might to convince himself it was only because he needed the money, Jake had to admit that something else was drawing him to this particular case. His client's concern and worry about Emma seemed to be genuine, and the police reports just didn't add up. Jake would never be sure whether it was these facts, or whether he was trying to relieve his conscious by making up for what had happened in the past, but, in the end, he had accepted the case.

Arriving in Cedar Falls, he managed to rent a small cabin whose property was adjacent to Emma's. Setting up a surveillance system consisting of cameras placed in the woods outside her farmhouse, Jake was able to transmit information back to the monitors and recorders that were set up in the cabin. For a few weeks or so, he was content to observe her, undetected, via the cameras, but, then his desire to watch her in person started to grow, taking over his good sense. Making sure to stay well hidden, he surveyed her from the safety of the trees. To Jake it was quite apparent that Emma treasured her seclusion, yet, at the same time, she appeared to be full of life. While working in her garden, she would sing, somewhat off key, and never failed to take time to feed the squirrels and rabbits. Jake was pretty sure, however, that feeding them was unnecessary as they seem to get their fill on their own, as Emma made no attempt to keep them out of the garden. He had also seen her comfortably visiting with neighbors and friends who would drop by. But, most of all, he enjoyed watching her when she sat alone in the golden glow of the early evening sunset, sitting in her old rocker on the front porch, looking so full of peace.

Jake now found himself getting bolder when he watched her in the mornings, standing almost in plain sight. With grey eyes, that were the color of the early morning fog that cloaked him, he followed her every move. A strong urge was developing within him to talk with her, and get to know her. He repeatedly told himself to keep it professional, but, something else pulled at him. Jake knew that she was now aware of him, as he had no doubt the dog had let her know he was out here. He'd seen both of them, in the mornings, peering out the window. The dog—her protector and constant companion.

The dog discovered him one morning, when Jake had been hiding in the trees. He hadn't heard the canine come up from behind, however, when Jake turned around to leave here was this big, black lab sitting there, staring at him with oddest, blue eyes he had ever seen in either man or animal. Choosing to just ignore him and walk away, Jake had hoped the dog would remain near home. That, as it turned out, was not the case. The dog followed him all the way back to the cabin, staying about ten to fifteen feet behind. After Jake went inside, the dog planted himself on the porch, and remained there for the entire afternoon. Then, right before dusk, he left. Jake had been certain that sooner or later the dog would have led Emma to him, but, so far he hadn't. The dog, Otis, whose name he had finally discovered on one of his tags, now came to see him on a regular basis. Otis also knew that Jake was there in the morning, standing in the mist rising off the creek. It was as if the dog was trying his best to bring Jake and Emma together.

Jake's thoughts turned back to his cameras, and he decided he needed to go make a routine check of them. As he opened the cabin door to leave, there sat the dog.

"Well, speak of the devil," Jake said. Otis happily wagged his tail.

# Chapter Five

Opening the door, Emma could see the Sheriff's car parked in her driveway. Deputy Sheriff Matt Green stood on her porch, hat in hand.

"So, Deputy Green, what brings you out this way?" Emma asked.

"Just came by to drop off this envelope from Henry. He said you'd need it to finish the work you were doin' for him."

Henry Griffith was Cedar Falls' only attorney. Emma had met him soon after moving to town. With his rotund figure, snow white hair and moustache, she thought he looked more like a Santa Claus—if he just had a beard—than a lawyer. His eyes sparkled with a kindness she noticed right off. Henry, however, had one of the best reputations statewide in the legal community. Finding out about Emma's background, Henry asked her if she would do most of his work, allowing her to work out of her home. Emma, who didn't need the money as she had become independently wealthy after Charles' death, agreed to work for him. She did so, in part to keep herself busy, but, also because she truly liked the old man. Disliking the fact that he had been forced into the computer age, Henry knew that sooner or later he was going to have to become a part of it, and was more than happy for Emma's assistance.

Emma gave Matt a cheery smile, "I was going to go into town a little later today to pick it up. You didn't need to go out of you way to bring it out here."

"That's okay. I was in the neighborhood." Emma noticed Matt appeared to be a little nervous, turning his hat over and over in his hand. He glanced around the yard, "So, where's Otis?"

"Oh, he took off a little earlier this morning. I haven't seen him for a while. He's probably visiting a girlfriend, or something. Would you like something to drink?"

"Yeah, that'd be nice."

"Well, have a seat and I'll be right back."

Emma went into the kitchen, and took a couple of glasses out of the cupboard, filling them with ice tea. She liked Matt. Getting to know him in the months since she moved here, Emma concluded he was a good person, and very well respected by the people in town. His lanky frame, brown curly hair, and dark brown eyes, which were surrounded by thick lashes, gave him an appealing boyish charm. Maggie, the owner of the Cedar Falls Café, told her that Matt was considered to be the most eligible bachelor in town. Maggie and Matt had known each other since junior high, and Maggie said she could always tell when Matt liked a girl. Emma had been somewhat embarrassed the day Maggie told her there was no doubt that Matt liked her. Although flattered by this news, Emma wasn't sure she was quite ready for any kind of relationship. Carrying the ice tea back out to the porch, she settled herself down into the oak rocker across from Matt.

"So, what's new in town?" she asked.

"Not much. Had a little excitement at Anderson's mortuary last night. Seems someone decided to steal one of the old coffins from out back. We figure it was just some kids gettin' their kicks."

"Well, Halloween's not too far off. Maybe someone's planning to have a big, spooky party."

"Wouldn't surprise me. So, how's everything goin' for you out here? Are you enjoyin' the place?"

"I love it. It's so peaceful and quiet. I suppose I would get lazy and dream the day away, if it wasn't for Henry."

Matt sat back and chuckled, "As long as computers are the wave of the future, Henry will definitely keep you busy. Sometimes I think he feels that they went too far inventing the electric typewriter."

Emma laughed, "I think you're right."

"Thanks again for the ice tea, but I guess I should get goin'. We had a couple of accidents in the fog this morning, and I need to go get some statements."

Matt's mention of the fog brought Emma's thoughts back to the stranger. Matt noticed the dark expression that passed over her face.

"Is somethin' wrong, Emma?" She could hear the concern in his voice.

Matt was fully aware of Emma's past situation, as she had checked in, upon her arrival, with the local authorities like she promised Detective Harris she would. Off and on, Matt was keeping in touch with Harris, and it bothered him that they were no closer to catching Hudson's killer, than when Emma had left Denver.

"I'm not sure," Emma hesitated for a moment. "No, not really, I guess."

"Are you sure nothin's wrong?"

"It's probably just my imagination, but—"

Their conversation was interrupted by several barks that pierced the air. Otis came tearing out of the woods, racing forward and sliding to a stop. He turned and looked back, ears alert, tail wagging so fast that he was swirling up the colorful autumn leaves all around his feet.

"Well, looks like Romeo's returned." Matt grinned.

Turning his head back to the house, Otis spotted Matt on the porch. After one more glance at the woods, Otis made a beeline toward the house. He trotted up on the porch, ignoring Emma, and sat down at Matt's feet.

"Well, good day to you too," Emma quipped. Otis looked at her as if to say, "I've already seen you today, but I haven't seen, Matt." Emma shook her head and smiled to herself. Otis was a good judge of character—after all he hadn't liked Charles—but, he did like Matt.

Matt scratched the dog's ears. "So, who's your girlfriend?" Otis just laid his head on Matt's lap, insisting on more attention.

"Don't feel too insulted," Emma said, "He won't tell me either." However, Emma had to wonder just who it was the dog was really visiting.

* * *

Jake was making the rounds of his camera equipment which had been strategically placed all around Emma's house. The fog had burned off, and the early afternoon sunshine felt warm on his back as it worked its way through the soft fabric of his shirt. Coming up on the camera which was focused on the front of the house, he heard a loud tapping sound coming from behind him. It sounded like short bursts from a jackhammer, though Jake had to admit it would be a small jackhammer. He swung around, not seeing see anything behind him. Otis, who had been following him all morning, was sitting at the base of a tree, staring intently toward the top. Following the dog's gaze up the tree, he spotted a large red headed woodpecker. The bird looked like a rock climber with no ropes, as he hung precariously from the tree's trunk by his toes. With focused determination, the bird was pecking away at the bark of the old oak. His head would bob up and down in quick, jerking motions, then he'd stop and look around, only to go back and start it all over again. Watching the bird, Jake had to wonder if the woodpecker would wind up with one hell of a headache later on.

Taking a few minutes to look around, he noticed just how beautiful these hills were. The scent of autumn was in the air, and the leaves were turning brilliant shades of red, orange, and gold. A small amount of dew still hung on the leaves, and as the gentle breeze played with the branches, they sparkled like jewels in the sun. Jake could see why Emma had moved here. These woods could make you forget about the outside world, if even for only a little while. Turning his attention back the camera he'd been checking, Jake noticed it appeared to have been knocked a little to one side.

"You think some little critter wanted his picture taken?" Jake said to the dog.

He knelt down and started to readjust the camera's position. Upon closer examination, he noticed that there was an extra hole that was in the ground. It appeared to be the same diameter as the rod inserted into the base of the camera, and was within three to four inches of where the equipment now sat. Someone else had been there. Jake hadn't seen anything unusual on the monitors earlier in the day, leaving him uncomfortable with the fact that whoever moved the camera had done so just since he left the cabin. Jake stood and carefully surveyed the area around the house and the woods behind him. Nothing appeared to be out of the ordinary. From first hand experience, however, Jake knew how easy it would be for someone to hide in these woods. Inspecting the camera to make sure that everything was still in working order, he made a mental note to review the video tapes as soon as he returned to the cabin. All of a sudden, Otis went sailing past him out of the woods, just as Jake heard laughter coming from Emma's porch.

From where he was in the trees, Jake had a full view of the house, and he noticed the Sheriff's car in the driveway. His immediate thought was Emma had been the one to find the camera, and had called in the police. He didn't think he had been that careless when he had set up the surveillance system. However, Jake became convinced, the longer he watched Emma and the Deputy, that they were no more aware of the surveillance system, than they were of his current presence. He had observed the Deputy there on several occasions, and it hadn't taken a rocket scientist to figure out he was there for more than business reasons. Several short barks brought Jake's attention back around to the dog. Otis was looking directly at him, trying his best to coax him out of the woods. Jake remained still, willing the dog to go up to the house. With one last look, Otis took off and promptly greeted the Deputy, as Emma's laughter once again filtered through the air.

The cozy picture taking place before him made Jake's stomach feel like lead. "This is ridiculous," he said to himself. "How can I be jealous over someone I don't even know." But, he was. Emma's laughter had a way of making him feel warm inside. Jake wanted to be the one up on that porch talking with her, seeing the sunshine bounce little lights of red and gold off her hair.

"I need a break here," Jake said as he shook his head trying to clear the images out of his mind. "Maybe I should just contact the client, tell 'em everything is okay, and finish up this damn job." But, then as he felt the weight of the camera in this hand, he realized that everything wasn't okay. Someone else had been fooling with his equipment, and he was now sure it wasn't Emma, or her Deputy friend. After repositioning the camera back to its original location, Jake began a search for anything that might tell him who had been there.

* * *

"Well, Emma, thanks again for the ice tea," Matt said, as he stepped off the porch.

"You're more than welcome. And, thank you for dropping the stuff off from Henry."

Matt started for his car, then turned around. "Uh, Emma,—"

"Yes."

"The town is having its Fall Festival on Saturday. They're gonna have booths, a fried chicken dinner, and a dance, and, well—" Matt's voice started to trail off.

Emma smiled at him teasingly, "Are you asking me for a date, Deputy Green?"

"Uh,…yeah."

"So, you weren't really just in the neighborhood when you dropped by today."

Matt was once again turning his hat over and over in his hand. He glanced up at Emma with his chocolate brown eyes. "No, not really."

"I would be more than happy to go with you, Matt."

A smile broke out across the Deputy's face. "That's great. I'll pick you up Saturday around eleven." Placing his hat on his head, he walked to the car.

Twinges of jealousy hit Jake again, and he frowned when he watched Emma smile and wave at the Deputy. Unaccustomed to these feelings he was having, Jake was trying to figure them out when he became sharply aware of another presence in the woods. It was someone, or something, that shouldn't have been there, and as Jake watched the Deputy drive away, so did it.

# Chapter Six

Emma went inside and put the glasses in the kitchen sink, tripping over Otis who had planted himself in the doorway.

"Well, you've had a busy morning, I see." Otis gazed up at her with a mischievous twinkle in his eye. "And, just what were you barking at? Wouldn't your girlfriend come and join you?" Otis shook his head as if answering her, but then proceeded to scratch behind one ear.

"I wish I knew where you went every day," she said, giving him a big hug. Emma knew it would be easy enough to find out if she could just get the courage to follow him. She just wasn't sure she really wanted to know. Convinced, now, that someone was watching her, Emma still hadn't pursued the matter with the authorities because the dog seemed unconcerned by this person's presence. Maybe she was being foolish by putting so much faith in a dog, but, she had to admit when it came to people Otis was a much better judge of character than she was. Perhaps this man was just a neighbor who didn't know exactly how to introduce himself. Perhaps one morning she would go out and say hello. Perhaps.

Emma picked up the manilla envelope Matt had delivered

from Henry, and headed to her desk. Slitting the top open, she pulled out two cassette tapes which would finish up the interrogatories she had been transcribing all week, and were due in court next Tuesday. Tomorrow was Friday, and Emma made a note on her desk calendar to get the finished product to Henry no later than mid-morning. The Saturday block on the calendar caught her eye, and she jotted down "Date with Matt." Emma was looking forward to her first date in a very long time.

\* \* \*

Jake walked the perimeter of the house while staying hidden in the trees, double checking all his cameras. None, but the one, appeared to have been tampered with. He tried to remain as quiet as possible, hoping to see a manifestation of the unseen force he had felt. Jake knew, without question, he was not alone in these woods, however, the thick coating of dew soaked leaves on the forest floor absorbed all sounds, and left little trace of any footprints. Someone, obviously, now knew that Emma was being watched over as they had discovered the surveillance equipment, but, Jake was also sure whoever it was had been unaware of his immediate presence. Coming around to the front of the house, he got the feeling whoever had been there earlier was gone. Could it have been is imagination? No. His gut told him he was not wrong, and he headed back to his cabin.

Pouring himself a cup of coffee, Jake sat down at the kitchen table. Most of the cabin's furnishings were of oak, much of them having been made by the Amish. Their lines were clean and neat, without much in the way of decorative extras. The kitchen table and chairs were simple, built for practicality. All the other furnishings, like the bed, dresser, and small tables, were of similar design, built to serve their specific purpose in life, with no fanfare.

However, in the living room there was a comfortable old couch and an overstuffed chair that sat on a big, multi-colored braided rug in front of the fireplace. On a number of nights, Jake had found himself stretched out on that couch, gazing into the fire, enjoying its warmth. The cabin was cozy and peaceful, and he enjoyed that feeling.

Booting up the laptop computer on the table, Jake clicked the mouse, and opened up his e-mail. Several messages appeared on the screen. A couple were from other investigators he networked with now and again, one was from an old friend with the Marshal's Service, and another from a corporate client he'd done business with in the past. At the bottom of the list was a message from the client who had hired him to watch Emma. He double clicked the message, and it opened up on the screen.

> *Dear Mr. McLean:*
> *I believe that Emma is still danger. If my suspicions are correct about who Charles' murderer is, then I think they may be headed your way. Once again, money is no concern, so I ask that you stay on the case, and continue to watch her. I will stay in touch.*

Jake's thoughts flew back to the camera, the e-mail confirming his suspicions that Emma was now being stalked. A protective instinct overwhelmed him, and Jake knew he would make sure no one could get to her. At the earliest opportunity, he would bug her house, and hide a couple of miniature cameras at the same time. Personal patrols of the grounds around the house would need to be stepped up also. A number of times, Jake had thought of just approaching her, telling her who he was, and what he was doing, but so far he hadn't. The client insisted that he keep his distance, at least until they had more proof regarding their suspicions because they didn't want to accuse an innocent person. Jake was beginning to question his client's line of reasoning, but, then again, they were paying the bills, and as a professional, he needed to respect their wishes.

Jake went through his black equipment bag, sorting out the audio bugs and cameras he would need to plant in the farmhouse. Emma loved her home, and the fact that she seemed to feel so safe and secure there started to nag his conscience. He was going to invade her privacy by turning it into a prison, where everything she said and did would be monitored.

"What the hell am I doing?" Jake grumbled to himself, running his hands through his dark hair.

Sitting back in his chair, Jake started having second thoughts about what he was planning to do. He wanted Emma to trust him, even if she didn't know he was there, and he feared if she ever found out it was he that had violated her sanctuary, she would hate him. Why should that bother him so much? This was just another job. But, somewhere deep inside he knew it was becoming more than that.

"I'm sorry, Em," Jake said, apologizing to the empty chair in front of him. "It's the only way I know of to keep you safe."

The rest of the afternoon was spent double checking equipment and packing it all into a padded knapsack which had been specifically designed to transport the sensitive equipment without damaging it. Jake wanted to make sure he had it with him every time he went to observe the house, so, when an opportunity arose for him to be able to get inside, he wouldn't have to come back to the cabin first. Jake also kept a close eye on the monitors receiving images from the perimeter cameras, seeing nothing unusual. Emma had spent the afternoon outside washing her car, squirting Otis with the hose. She was laughing as the dog picked up the hose in his mouth, running after her, squirting her back.

Later, Jake watched her hang out some laundry to dry. He didn't think, in this modern day and time, anyone did that anymore. Didn't everyone use a dryer? Picking up his knapsack, he closed the door behind him.

Walking out onto the creaking boards of the front porch, he deeply inhaled the sweet fall air. Though there was getting to be a chill in the morning air, the October afternoons were still sunny and warm. The sun was starting to move down to the western horizon, as the earth's atmosphere shifted from blue to gold. Stepping off the porch, he headed down the path to the stream.

\* \* \*

Emma's day had been a wonderful one. Matt had asked her for a date. She'd finished the interrogatories for Henry, and had even gotten around to washing and waxing her car, which was a great accomplishment, since she'd been used to those full-service car washes in Denver. Lastly, she had done her laundry, hanging it outside to dry. Emma loved the smell her clothes could only get from the sunshine—a fresh, sweet smell that she remembered from her childhood, before her mother got a dryer. That memory touched something precious inside of her. She loved her childhood, and wondered sometimes why she had ever had to grow up.

Sitting in her favorite rocker on the covered porch of the farmhouse, Emma watched the golden glow take over everything in its path. She decided that being a grown-up might be okay after all, otherwise, she wouldn't have a date on Saturday with the town's most eligible bachelor. Emma laughed at herself. It felt good to laugh again, it had been a long time. She hadn't laughed much during her marriage, and thought back to the night that Charles died.

They'd been attending a political fund raiser for Charles' mayoral campaign. Charles had gotten in a heated discussion with Adam Shepard, senior partner of Denver's largest law firm, and someone who could have been one of his biggest backers. Emma didn't know what the argument was about, but, being the good wife of a political candidate, decided to try to smooth the ruffled waters. She'd proceeded to soothe Alan's bruised ego and, in the end, he'd left a sizable contribution. However, her intervention had only brought out the worst in Charles who, in his arrogant and condescending manner, had disciplined her not only in front of his campaign staff, but, a number of other contributors. He'd almost slapped her when Emma tried to explain why she had spoken with Adam. What bothered her most, though, was she had stood there, totally embarrassed, taking his wrath in silence.

David, who had been Charles' campaign manager from the beginning, came to her rescue. He had gotten Charles off to the side, out of everyone's earshot, including Emma's. However, from the expressions on both of their faces, she could tell the conversation was taking a nasty turn.

"What the hell do you think you're doing? Emma was just trying to keep you're ass out of trouble." David's tone made it apparent that he was furious with Charles.

"I don't need her help." Charles snapped back. "She's here simply as a decoration on my arm, and she needs to keep her fucking mouth shut."

"We need Adam's political support, as well as his money. If it hadn't been for Emma, we'd have lost it."

"I can handle Adam."

"Well, you sure as hell didn't tonight." David said through gritted teeth. "Look, I'm your campaign manager, and I'm telling you we can't afford any more of your temper tantrums. You need to present a happy home front, if you want to win this thing."

Charles' eyes darkened with anger. "You may run my campaign, David, but not my marriage. I'm still her husband, and I'll treat Emma as I see fit. You just mind your own damn business."

"You really are an ass, Charles. You don't even realize what you have in Emma. She's a beautiful, caring woman, and she sure as hell deserves better than you."

At first a look of shock crossed Charles' face, but then he flashed a vicious smile at David. "So, that's it. You're in love with her. You're in love with my wife."

When David didn't answer, Charles continued, "Well, in light of this new info, I'll be expecting your resignation on my desk in the morning. After all, it wouldn't look very good for my campaign manager, and employee, to be sniffing around after my wife, would it?"

David locked eyes with Charles. "Are you threatening me, Charles?"

"Let's just say if you know what's good for you, and what's good for Emma, you'll be leaving town."

David stepped forward, his ice blue eyes piercing into Charles' face. "Let's just say if you hurt Emma one more time, you won't live to regret it."

Emma had been watching the exchange between the two men. When Charles turned and looked at her, the rage in his face was terrifying. He then turned and stormed out of the hotel ballroom, leaving Emma to pick up the pieces, and close the fund raiser down. David came over, offering his apologies, but, stumbling somewhat over his words. His eyes betrayed what his words could not tell her. She reached up, pushing his golden hair out of his eyes, and kissed him on the cheek. The look she gave him told him she appreciated his support and understanding. Emma was sure he would've preferred her to leave with him, but he was, as always, a gentleman. David gave her a kind, reassuring look, gently kissed her lips, and left.

Charles' abrupt departure had left Emma stranded at the hotel. By the time she had made apologies to all of their guests, settled up with the hotel management, and gotten a cab home, it was nearly two o'clock in the morning. She had not been prepared for what she found that freezing December night.

A low, rumbling growl brought Emma back to the porch. She hated remembering that night, and was frustrated with herself for allowing those memories to invade her wonderful day. Night was settling in, although she could still make out the shadows of the trees as they tried their best to blend in with the oncoming darkness. Another growl reached her ears, and she looked down at Otis. The dog's attention was fixated on the trees that lined the road leading to the house. His ears were back, and the soft, wavy fur on his neck had started to rise.

"What's wrong, Oats? What do you see?" Emma asked, her eyes scanning the woods where he was looking. Again he growled. She began to feel uncomfortable, looking harder for some sign of movement in the trees. All of a sudden, Otis' head whipped around and he looked toward the path leading to the stream. His ears pricked forward, and there was a slight wag to his tail. Emma's gaze went to the path, but, it seemed just as empty as the woods by the road. When she looked back at Otis, he appeared to be watching a tennis match. First he would look at the road, emitting a soft growl from his throat, then he would look toward the path as if he expected a knight in shining armor to appear. Her apprehension was growing. The dog didn't appear to be afraid of one of the entities, but, he had a definite concern about the other, and Emma, at this point, didn't care for either of them. Standing up, she walked over to the top step where Otis was standing. Kneeling down beside him, she encircled his warm neck.

"How about we call it a night, huh?" Otis turned towards her, then back at the woods. Emma scratched his ears, then stood, opening the squeaky screen door, allowing Otis to trot in ahead of her. The dog promptly jumped up on the couch, continuing to stare out the window. Emma took one last look at the darkening woods and closed the door.

\* \* \*

Jake had been admiring her from his hiding place in the trees. The bronze light of the setting sun surrounded her as she rocked on the porch, seemingly oblivious to the world around her. Through a pair of high powered binoculars, he focused in on her face. Emma's skin was the color of cream, with a slight blush to her cheeks. Her delicate pink lips were curled up in a peaceful smile. Jake wanted to reach out and touch her, anticipating how soft her skin would feel under his hands, and how sweet she would taste to his lips. The thought about just ending this charade, and telling her who he was, crossed his mind, as he continued to watch her. Then Jake noticed a dark, haunted expression float across her face. Whatever she was thinking about looked as if it frightened her, and that bothered him. No one should have to be feeling the fears that seem to be possessing her. Was this fear something from her past, or a new fear that she now possessed?

Jake lowered the binoculars and bent down to get a candy bar out of his bag. He planned on sticking around for a while tonight, and he was getting a little hungry. Before heading back to the cabin, he wanted to make sure Emma was safe and secure inside the house. When Jake stood back up, he noticed Otis was standing at the head of the steps staring toward the road. Focusing the binoculars on the dog, Jake noticed his ears where laid back, and the fur was up on his neck. Swinging the binoculars in the direction of the road, he searched the woods for anything that seemed out of place. With the shadows squeezing out the sunlight, it was hard to make out any kind of movement. Jake glanced back at the porch and locked onto those midnight blue eyes that were looking directly at him. Somehow, it never ceased to amaze him how the dog always knew where he was. Otis turned away toward the road, then back at Jake. They both knew that something was out there, something that shouldn't be, something dangerous.

Jake focused in one more time on Emma. He could see the uneasiness on her face, as she surveyed the woods. He wanted to reassure her that everything would be okay, that he was here for her. She walked over to the dog, giving him a hug, and then went inside. Even before Emma had shut the door, Jake noticed the dog was already looking out the window. A few seconds later, he was joined by Emma. They remained there for a few moments, looking out at the darkness. Jake settled in for what he anticipated to be a long night, as Emma pulled down the old-fashioned shade.

# Chapter Seven

A dry rustling sound caused Jake to stir. The musty smell of damp hay reached his nose and he shook himself awake. He'd spent the night in Emma's barn, refusing to leave the house unguarded. Thin streams of sunlight were making their way through the cracks in the boards. The early morning air was clear and crisp. Jake rose, feeling the stiffness in what seemed like every muscle of his body. It had been a long time since he had slept out on the ground. From the loft above, a small tuft of hay fell on his head. Turning his face upward, he saw the small grey head of a squirrel peering over the edge, chattering at him, as if scolding him for sleeping late.

"Yeah, yeah, I'm getting up." The squirrel bounded off, causing more hay to fall on Jake's head. Brushing his fingers through his hair, he dislodged the pieces of hay entangling themselves in the dark strands. He could feel smaller pieces falling down the back of his shirt. Walking toward the barn door, Jake untucked his shirt, shaking it out. Gazing out at the woods, he wondered if they were being watched. He didn't think so.

After Emma had gone inside last night, Jake had investigated the area of the woods that had caught the dog's attention. Using night vision binoculars to scan the area, he thought he'd seen someone, or something, headed through the woods toward the main road. He attempted to follow them, but, the darkness and the prickly underbrush around the trees made the going difficult. Upon reaching the road, Jake had found it empty. Whoever was watching Emma was now not only aware of Jake's surveillance system, but, that he was making a point of guarding her in person. Maybe that knowledge would make them reluctant to return, however, he couldn't help remembering what his client had said. Jake didn't want to put Emma in more danger, however, knew he couldn't protect her from just the confines of the cabin anymore.

His gaze drifted over to the house. Emma was up. The back door was open and the tantalizing smell of fresh coffee and sizzling bacon floated towards him over a light breeze. Jake's stomach rumbled, begging him for some kind of sustenance. The candy bar from the night before had not exactly been a satisfying dinner. Now that he knew she was all right, he needed to get back to the cabin. Picking up the knapsack, Jake was about to step out of the barn when Emma walked out on the back deck. She was bundled up in a big, green, terry cloth robe, which seemed to swallow her up. Cradling a steaming cup of coffee in her hands, she perched on the top step of the deck. The soft curls of Emma's tousled hair outlined her face, as she turned it up toward the sun, drinking in its warmth. She appeared to be more relaxed this morning. Jake's stomach rumbled again, the delicious odors from the house making his mouth water.

* * *

Emma turned when she heard the screen door open behind her. A black nose slowly peeked out as Otis pushed his way through onto the deck. He lowered his front paws, sticking his rear end in the air, stretching, then shook himself from head to tail. Padding over, he sat down by her.

"Well, you finally decided to get up, huh?" Emma ruffled his ears. The dog had still been asleep on her bed when she came downstairs earlier. Even though he took up most of the bed, he was always allowed to sleep with her. She enjoyed the extra warmth he provided, and felt more secure just knowing he was there. That had been especially true last night. Emma wasn't sure what, or who, had been out there, but, for the first time since she'd moved in had locked all her doors and windows, even pulling down every shade in the house. It had taken some time for her to fall asleep, however, once she had, she slept deeply.

This morning was beautiful, and Emma felt much more at ease. The air was cool, but not uncomfortably so. She liked sitting out here with her coffee, listening to the birds and watching the wildlife. She began to think that perhaps all that had upset Otis last night had been nothing more than some animal. The dog seemed fine this morning, ignoring everything except the bacon on her plate.

"Don't you know that bacon's not good for you?" Otis looked her in the eye, making her feel guilty.

"What?!" He huffed at her, as if to question why she was eating it then.

They both eyed the plate of bacon, looking back at each other. "Okay, we might as well ruin our health together." Emma picked up a strip of bacon, tossing it to the dog, who caught it in mid-air, and she munched on another piece. Emma didn't fix bacon very often, but loved the smell of it while it was frying, and savored the salty taste. After last night, this morning had seemed like a good one to fix it.

"You want to go for a ride into town with me this morning, or do you have other plans?" Emma asked. At the word "ride", Otis' ears pricked forward, and he bounded off the steps, running circles around the teal green Jeep parked next to the house.

Emma started laughing, "Not, yet. I still have to take a shower and get dressed. Can't go in my bathrobe, you know." The dog stopped by the passenger's door and planted himself there. He made it obvious he was not about to move, letting her know she was going nowhere without him.

"I get the message. But, you're going to be sitting there for a while." Emma chuckled as she went back inside, knowing that he would still be in that same spot when she returned.

\* \* \*

Jake leaned his shoulder against the frame of the barn door. So, she was going to town. This would be the perfect morning to be able to get into the house, and it should only take him around fifteen minutes to plant the needed equipment. Settling back, he waited for her to leave.

A short time later, a movement from the upstairs window caught his eye. Emma was standing at the open window. Her robe was tied in a loose knot at the waist, and hung slightly open. She was combing through her freshly washed hair, and he could see water droplets sparkling in the light as they slowly trickled down from the top of her partially revealed breasts to the valley between them. Jake felt a tightening sensation in his groin. Still chilled from the night before, he pictured himself with her in a hot, steamy shower, his skillful hands sliding over her silken, wet body. There were a number of ways he could think of to dry those water droplets off her body and, afterwards, would massage the lavender scented body lotion she wore over every inch of her delicate skin. His imagination was so real that Jake's fingers tingled, as if he was touching something fine and soft. A slight nudge at his fingertips brought him back to reality. Looking down he saw a black, furry nose demanding his attention.

"Well, I suppose you wonder what I'm doing here." Otis glanced up at the window where Emma had been standing, and then back at Jake. "I just wanted to make sure you two were all right. We both know that there was something out there last night that shouldn't have been." The dog let out a little whine, looking toward the woods. "Whoever it was left shortly after you went inside, and I thought I'd hang around a while. I haven't felt them out there today though, have you?" Otis cocked his head to one side, appearing to agree with him. Looking at the confident expression on the dog's face, it dawned on Jake just who he was having a conversation with.

"What the hell am I doing? I'm standing here talking to a dog. Jake, you're in bad need of a reality check. Guess I'd better start talking to some people pretty soon, or I'll lose all my social skills, and I don't have that many to start with." Otis gave him a curious look, as Jake continued to mutter to himself.

A few minutes later, they heard the back door of the farmhouse slam shut. Emma called out for the dog. "Oats, where are you? Come on, we've gotta go." Otis started toward the door, and Jake fell back into the shadows. He was able to see her standing by the jeep. Emma had put on some snug fitting jeans, and a sunny, yellow tank top, all of which showed off the sexy, little figure that lay beneath. Her medium length chestnut hair glowed in the sun, and hung in little waves around the back of her neck.

Emma called out again, "Otis, get your butt out here, or I'm leaving without you." The dog started out the barn door, then turned around looking at Jake, waiting for him to follow.

"Not today, big guy, I've got other plans. You'd better get going though, or she's going to go without you." Otis trotted off, leaping up onto the passenger's seat of the Jeep. Jake watched Emma slide her shapely legs behind the wheel, and drive down the oak lined lane leading to the main road.

Approaching the back of the house, Jake could see why she loved this place, it had a lot of character. It was a two story, stone farmhouse with white shutters, a back deck, and a covered front porch. Nature had added its own accent with a vine that was climbing its way up the side of the house. The vine, which in the summer was a vibrant green, had turned a fiery red as the oncoming autumn took over. Boards on the deck creaked under his feet as he reached the door. The knob was old-fashioned brass, with a skeleton keyhole. Jake turned the handle, expecting the door to open easily, but, it was locked. Since he had started watching Emma, her habit had been to leave the doors unlocked and the windows open. He searched the outside of the house, discovering that every window was closed, even those on the second floor. Jake walked around to the front door, finding it not only locked, but, secured by the dead bolt. Returning to the back door, he pulled a small leather case from his knapsack, unzipping it. Several thin, silver tools lay neatly inside. Selecting a tool from the case, Jake inserted it in the keyhole, turning it until he heard a familiar click. Returning the tool to its case, he entered the house.

The kitchen was large, like those in a lot of older farmhouses. The feel of families gathered for meals, and smells of home cooking hung in the air. The large, well worn oak table and chairs in the middle of the floor didn't even come close to filling up the room. White cabinets, with glass panels in the doors, lined the upper walls. Blue and white print curtains matched the subtle blue marble patterned linoleum on the floor. Sun shone through the windows gleaming off the oak counter tops adding a cheery, brightness to the room.

Jake made his way into the living room. A braided rug of

creams and browns partially covered the polished wood floors. The hutch, end tables, and bookcases were a deep polished mahogany, and appeared to be quite old. Emma's T.V. cabinet was made from an antique armoire that had been converted with shelves for the DVD and stereo components. Near the side window was a roll top desk. A computer monitor sat in the middle, with files stacked along one side. Upon examining the desk, Jake realized this was also an antique that Emma had converted to fit her needs. Besides the computer, the only other modern furnishings were a pellet stove, and a big comfortable couch that sat underneath the front window. The paintings on the walls ranged from water colors of old houses, to lighthouses, to a picture of a dog curled up on a bed. He knew that painting to be one of Andrew Wyeth's, but, couldn't recall the title.

Jake sifted through the files on the desk, noting that most of them were case files from Henry Griffith's law office. Every cubby hole in the old desk was filled with some kind of office supplies. Most of the desk drawers contained personal and business files, however, in the top drawer he found her address book. Flipping through it, Jake was surprised to find that it was not nearly as full as he had anticipated. With the prominent social life her husband had had in Denver, he thought that it would have been filled with a lot of social friends and contacts. Instead, the book contained mainly her family, and what was probably a few close friends. Inside the front of the book was a pink sticky note with "important 31483736342" written on it. Jake jotted down the number on another sticky note and tucked it into his shirt pocket, replacing the address book back where he had found it.

A search of the rest of the main floor revealed a small spare bedroom off the back of the house, as well as a guest bath. Jake then turned his attention to the second floor. At the top of the stairs was a large bathroom which, unlike most of the downstairs, was very modern. There was a long counter top with double sinks, a large, spacious shower, and a Jacuzzi tub that had a green house window right beside it. Emma had decorated the bath in soft shades of green. Plants, both potted and hanging, surrounded the Jacuzzi. Jake imagined that it must feel like being in a pool in the middle of the forest. He wouldn't mind relaxing in those bubbles himself, with some company of course.

Emma's bedroom was his last stop. The room was like Emma herself—warm, soft, and very feminine. Small bouquets of lilacs were woven into the comforter and curtains. There were accent pillows of lavender and cream tossed on the bed. The rest of the furnishings were simple, just a dressing table, chest of drawers, night stand, and carved headboard, all made out of deep cherry wood. The scent of lavender hung in the air.

Surveying the room, Jake made the decision to plant the listening device underneath the Victorian lamp on the night stand. The best place to put the miniature camera appeared to be in the overhead light fixture, which would allow him to see most of the room. He would be able to watch her while she slept, curled up under her lilac comforter, and see the gentle morning sun kiss her eyes, waking her to a new day. Jake's imagination kicked in, and he thought how she would look when, after her shower, her robe would fall by her feet on the floor, leaving her standing naked in front of the mirror. He was sure the body she possessed was both beautiful and sensuous. This camera was going to afford him the opportunity to be a part of the most intimate details of her life.

Reaching towards the light fixture, Jake's hand froze. An uncomfortable, almost dirty feeling came over him. He was invading her privacy to an extent that he wasn't sure he wanted to. Was he certain he really needed to have a camera right in the bedroom? Jake wanted to make sure that no one was going to get up the stairs without him seeing. If he put the camera in the ceiling fan in the hall, he would be able to cover the stairs and the hallway leading to the bedroom. The part of his mind that wanted to be close to her tried to convince Jake to put the camera back in the bedroom. If he did so, it would almost be like he was here with her. Jake squeezed his eyes shut, cursing under his breath. This case, and this woman, were getting to him. He just hoped it would be over soon. Frustrated, he hid the camera in the ceiling fan, and went downstairs.

Jake planted two more bugs, one in the roll top desk, and one under the kitchen table. While in the kitchen, he replaced the smoke detector with one that contained a small camera. The back door was going to be the easier one for someone to break into, especially since Emma had seen fit to start using the dead bolt out front. Jake picked up his knapsack, locking the back door behind him as he left. He wanted to stay, he liked the feeling inside her house—one hundred percent Emma. However, right now he needed to get to town. Jake sprinted across the yard to the path, heading back to the cabin, and his truck.

# Chapter Eight

Emma wheeled her Jeep Wrangler into the parking space in front of Henry Griffith's office. She grabbed the manilla envelope from under the passenger's seat, where she had put it to keep it from blowing out. The morning was warming up, and she'd taken the top off the Jeep, loving the feeling of the wind on her face. Emma popped in the front door of the old brick building, Otis at her heels. Henry looked up from his desk, and smiled. He was happy to see her, his day always seemed to go better after one of Emma's visits.

Otis headed straight for Henry, knowing the old man would have a treat for him. He sat down politely at Henry's feet, holding a paw up for him to shake. With good manners that the lawyer would have shown his most important clients, Henry leaned over, taking the big, black paw in his hand, giving it a firm shake. He then formally addressed the dog.

"Good morning, Mr. Otis, and what can I do for you today?" Otis' gaze went to the top drawer of the credenza that was behind Henry's chair.

"You know, I do believe that I have something here for you," Henry chuckled, as he fished out a cookie from the drawer, placing it on the floor. Otis' head was bent down toward the cookie, but he eyes looked up, waiting for Henry's next move. They both knew the drill well, and even though the cookie smelled unbelievably good to his sensitive nose, Otis waited with patience for Henry's signal. With a twinkle in his crystal blue eyes, and the start of smile spreading on his lips, Henry gave the dog a slight nod. Without waiting for any confirmation, Otis snapped up the cookie, devouring it in one bite.

Emma burst out laughing. "Henry, you've got him well trained. He's not that polite with me when he wants something at home."

Henry grinned, "Otis and I have reached a compromise. After all, I am an attorney, and that's what attorney's do, compromise."

"Well, I don't know if it is a compromise or not, but, you do have an understanding," Emma said as she watched Otis sniffing around the floor for any tiny particle of cookie that might have escaped his clutches. "I just wanted to bring in those interrogatories that were due. I'd be happy to make the copies and then take them over to the Fed Ex drop for you."

"I'd love it if you would make the copies for me. That blasted machine doesn't like me, and the copies I made yesterday are almost unreadable." Henry grumbled, giving the old copier that was standing in the corner a spiteful look.

Emma walked over to the copier and set the papers in the feeder tray. She looked at the control panel and noticed the words "ADD TONER" were flashing in the lower corner. Trying to suppress a laugh, she turned to Henry, "You know, Henry, one of these days you really need to learn how to add toner to this thing. What are you going to do when I'm not around anymore?"

Henry looked at her, stating matter-of-factly, "I'll probably go finagle copies out the girls at the Sheriff's Office like I did before. They always made copies for me, until I could get someone over here to fix the blasted thing."

Shaking her head and smiling, Emma replenished the copier's ink supply, and made the necessary copies. She sat down at the small reception desk that Henry had put in a corner of the office. Originally bought to make the office appear more formal, the desk now just served as another place for Henry to put things. Clearing off a little spot, she got the Fed Ex envelope out the drawer and started filling it out.

"Uh, Emma…you don't have to mail that for me. I'm going to run it over to Springfield this afternoon."

"Oh? I thought it didn't need to be filed until next Tuesday. I'm sorry, was I late getting this back to you?" Emma asked. She'd been sure she had given herself plenty of time to get the work done.

"No, you're right, it's not due until next Tuesday, but I've…uh…I've got some other things to take care of over there today." Emma noticed the old man's cheeks as they started to turn a rosy pink.

"So, when do I get to meet her?"

"What?! What are you talking about?" The stunned look on Henry's face told Emma she was right. The old lawyer had found himself a girlfriend.

"Oh, come on, Henry. You've spent more time in Springfield in the last two months, than since I met you. And, whenever you come back from there, you act like you're floating on air. So, who is she?" Emma teased.

Henry knew he'd been had, and that Emma would pester him until he gave it up. "I met her at the courthouse. She's one of the judges' secretaries, been there a long time. She helped me out on that Stonehill case, while the judge was out sick. We got to talking, and found out we had a lot in common."

"Okay. So, like I said, when do I get to meet her?"

"If you're a good girl, maybe tomorrow night."

"Are you bringing her to the fall festival tomorrow?" Emma asked, excitement in her voice. "That would be wonderful, Henry."

"Well, I'm going to ask her to come, don't know if she will or not."

"Oh, she will. How could she refuse an invitation from such a suave and debonair man as yourself?" Emma giggled.

Feeling somewhat embarrassed, Henry simply said, "We'll see."

Emma placed the copies of the interrogatories in an envelope for Henry, putting them in the only uncluttered spot in the office, which was a small table near the door.

"Henry, the envelope is right here by the door. Do you need anything else before I take off?"

"Don't think so. Thanks for all your help, and I'll probably see you Monday."

"Don't you mean tomorrow?" Emma teased him again.

He gave her an exasperated smile. "I'm sure you must have other people to annoy. And, take this cookie monster with you."

Emma left Henry's office and headed down the street toward the Cedar Falls Café. As was typical of many Midwestern towns, Cedar Falls was built around a town square. Most of the store fronts were weathered wood and brick, and looked like they probably hadn't changed in a hundred years. The square served as the town park, and in the middle there was a gazebo big enough to support the local town band. A number of the townspeople were setting up their booths of crafts and games for tomorrow's festival. There was a large tent in which the food would be served, along with tables and chairs for dining. A dance was to follow, and one of the local construction companies was busy building a wooden platform to serve as a dance floor. The colorful leaves on the oak trees enhanced the other fall decorations of hay bales, corn stalks, scarecrows, and pumpkins that were being placed throughout the park.

Emma was looking forward to tomorrow. She had always wanted to attend a small town festival and experience the uniqueness that could be found only there. By now she knew a lot of people in town, and was beginning to feel a part of things. With Matt having lived here most of his life, she was sure they would have a good time. A strange feeling came over her, a sixth sense of sorts, as she looked across the park, telling her that tomorrow might not be what she was expecting.

Entering the café, she left Otis to sunbathe himself on the bench outside. Most of the time, the little restaurant wasn't very busy at this time of the morning, however, due to the preparations for the festival going on across the street, almost all of the tables were full. Emma surveyed the counter for an empty stool, spotting one beside Matt Green. Must be her lucky day, she thought.

Emma walked up behind Matt, tapping him on the shoulder. "Excuse me, is this seat taken?"

A mixture of surprise and happiness filled Matt's eyes when he looked up and saw Emma standing beside him. Glancing around the café, he said, "Well, my girlfriend just left, and I don't think she's coming back, so I guess the seat's yours."

Emma gave him an affectionate smile, and sat down at the counter. "Buy a girl a cup of coffee?"

"Kind of pushy aren't you?" he grinned.

"Never know unless you ask."

"Maggie," Matt motioned to the waitress at the end of the counter, "Could I get a cup of coffee for this beautiful creature that just wandered in?"

Emma started to blush, as the curvy, red headed waitress made her way toward them with a fresh pot of coffee. Maggie O'Hara had worked at the café most of her life. It had been in her family for generations, and though her father was still the official owner, there was no doubt that Maggie was the one in charge. Even dressed in worn blue jeans and a white T-shirt with "Cedar Falls Café" silk-screened in purple in the upper, right-hand corner, she was a striking woman. She had the full, supple curves of a Greek statute, and her reddish-auburn hair set off her ivory skin. Those deep lavender colored eyes let you know that when dealing with her she was nobody's fool, and was a tough business woman. But, through the many conversations that Emma and Maggie had had, Emma knew that in the depths of those eyes there was also a woman full of romance. A woman who would make someone a wonderful wife. A woman she suspected was in love with Matt Green.

Emma's embarrassment was as much due to this fact, as to Matt's previous comment. She and Maggie were friends, and Maggie had never dissuaded her from becoming involved with Matt. Maggie knew how Matt felt about Emma, and only wanted happiness for them both. But, Emma was sure that Maggie wished things were different.

"I'm sorry, ma'am, is this guy botherin' you?" Maggie joked as she poured Emma's coffee. "If he is, I'll be glad to call the Sheriff's Office for ya."

Emma smiled. Maggie always knew how to make her feel comfortable in these awkward moments. "I guess he's not bothering me too much, especially since he's paying."

"Well, he may be paying for your coffee, but I'll tell you a secret. He's a lousy tipper."

"Now wait a minute," Matt defended himself, "I always leave you fifty cents in the morning, and that's just for a cup of coffee."

"A cup of coffee? Don't you mean more like a couple of pots?" Maggie bantered back.

"Well, I guess I'd better be goin' then. Don't want you runnin' out on my account." Matt got up from his stool, leaving a five on the counter. "That should cover the damages I think."

"That might even cover a cup to go, if ya want."

"Think I'll take that offer." Matt said. Turning to Emma, he gave her a peck on the cheek, "And, I'll see you tomorrow afternoon."

Blushing again, Emma said "I'm really looking forward to it. It should be a lot of fun."

Picking up his coffee, Matt nodded at Maggie, as he headed out the door. "See ya later for dinner, Maggie."

"We're having meat loaf," she called out after him.

Matt lived alone, and since the Sheriff's Office staff was small and his hours could be erratic he ate most of his meals at the café.

Turning her attention to Emma, Maggie said, "So, I see you've accepted Matt's invitation to our festival and dance."

"Yeah. He came over yesterday, on the pretense of delivering something for Henry. Took him a while to spit it out though."

"He's like that when he's nervous. He can talk up a blue streak most of the time, but, get him around a woman that he likes and sometimes he can't put two sentences together." Maggie laughed. "He's been like that since we were in high school."

One of the regular customers approached the counter, and Maggie stepped over in front of the register, chatting with him as she took care of his check. Emma sipped on her coffee, enjoying the homey atmosphere of the café. Almost everyone in here knew each other, and had welcomed Emma with open arms. Maggie had a way of making everyone in her restaurant feel at home. Emma had no doubt that with Maggie's intelligence and determination—she had graduated with honors from the University of Missouri—she would have made it big in the corporate world, but understood why she had chosen to remain here.

Maggie came back over to where Emma was sitting. "Need a refill?"

"No. I already had some this morning, so this should be plenty. Are you going to the festival?"

"I wouldn't miss it. Seems like something interesting always happens at these things. Last year they caught Buddy Graves makin' out with Jeanette Miller behind the library. Needless to say, Mr. Miller wasn't too thrilled." Maggie loved filling Emma in on the people in town. Emma speculated that she had gotten to know everyone so quickly, because of Maggie's stories.

"Well, it will be a new experience for me. And, I'm sure Matt will show me a good time."

"Matt's a good guy, even if I do give him a hard time now and then."

"Now and then?" Emma gave Maggie a mock look of astonishment.

"All right, maybe, most of the time, but he's still a good guy. He's a hard worker, well respected, kind, sincere, and—" Maggie voice started to trail off.

"And, pretty good looking, too, right?" Emma said, raising up her cup for another sip of coffee.

"As good looking as Otis' friend out there?" Maggie asked. Emma looked up to find Maggie staring out the window. Following Maggie's gaze over to the bench where she had left the dog, Emma found herself speechless. It was him, she knew it was, standing there scratching Otis' chest and talking to him. He lifted his head, looking straight at Emma, locking eyes with her through the plate glass window. Part of his face was obscured by the big red letters painted on the cafe's window, but she could clearly make out his eyes, which held hers with a paralyzing force. They remained this way for what seemed like several minutes, and Emma could feel the rest of the world dissolve in a blur around her. She could make out nothing else, but, the pair of intense eyes that seem to burn their way into the center of her being.

"Emma, do you know him?" Emma could hear Maggie's voice coming to her from afar. "Emma? Emma, are you okay?" Maggie tried again, finally penetrating the veil that had, just seconds before, surrounded her.

Emma blinked, and returned her attention to Maggie, she swallowed hard. "Yeah, I'm okay. I just—"

"Do you know him?"

"Uh, no," she paused, "No, I don't." It wasn't exactly a lie. She didn't really know him, and something told her not to tell anyone about him. Not just yet anyway.

"Well, I sure wish I did. I've gotta say, whoever he is, he's gorgeous."

Turning back to the window, Emma found that the only thing looking back at her was a black, furry face.

# Chapter Nine

The eyes watched her from the shadows of the trees in the park. They had followed her since her arrival in town, and now locked onto her as she left the café. Puzzled, she was scanning the street for the stranger who had been there just minutes ago. If they wanted to, they could tell her where he was. Inform her he was now watching her from the safety of his truck that was parked in front of the general store a few doors down, but, they wouldn't. The game they were playing was more fun, and their plan was coming together nicely. They were aware that Emma's self-proclaimed guardian was becoming quite attracted to her, and had stepped up his protection of her a little more each day. He had progressed from just a parameter electronic surveillance of her house, to personal patrols, including spending the night in her barn, to now a personal surveillance of her every move. The growing attachment of Emma's guardian to protect her day and night, added some risk to their plan, but, it hadn't been unexpected, and they welcomed the challenge.

The Deputy was another matter, however. The eyes had personally experienced the exchange between the Deputy and Emma at her house the other day, and realized more than a professional interest existed there. They'd seen him again today, at the counter in the café, sitting with her and giving her a kiss before he left. Something needed to be done. His interest in Emma had not been expected, and would not be tolerated.

The eyes continued to follow Emma as she walked back to her Jeep. She continued to search the buildings and park, still trying to find him. After one final glance around the square, she and the dog climbed into the Jeep, heading back out of town toward home. A few moments later, a dark blue, Dodge truck pulled out from in front of the general store and followed her. The eyes smiled. Their plan was working.

# Chapter Ten

The sound of heavy rain reverberated in the small cabin. Jake had just made it back from Emma's before the dark clouds let loose with sheets of water. He'd been glad that he'd planted the cameras in her house that morning, because the driving rain had made it almost impossible for him to see the outside of the farmhouse through the perimeter cameras. Being able to see and hear her, safe and warm inside, had eased his mind. He hadn't looked forward to another night in her barn, suspecting that the old building probably leaked.

Jake spent the evening watching Emma on the surveillance system. She'd fixed herself a wonderful dinner, consisting of a big tossed salad, fresh baked bread, corn, and a broiled steak. Thankful that his spy equipment didn't include "smell-a-vision," his own dinner, which was a bologna sandwich, had paled in comparison. After dinner, Jake had lost sight of her as she entered the living room, although he could still hear her. The consistent clicking of her fingers on the keyboard of her computer came through steady for the next couple of hours. A little while later, she appeared in the kitchen again, and poured herself a glass of white wine. He watched her disappear once more into the living room, and all was quiet.

Jake was beginning to feel uneasy. He hadn't heard anything for almost an hour. No movement, no sound, not even the T.V., which had been on most of the evening. Nothing but silence. Just as he started to berate himself for not installing a third camera, he heard her laugh and relief flooded through his body. Pretending to scold Otis, Emma said, "Get that ball out of the middle of my book, please." She had been reading. The sound of something hitting the floor came through the speaker.

"I don't want your nose in my book either. What? Are you bored?" she asked. Jake heard a small bark, and then the bouncing of a ball across the floor. Watching the monitor, he saw the ball roll into the kitchen, followed by a black blur. Jake couldn't help but laugh out loud as the big dog tried to stop on the linoleum, sliding almost to the back door. Retrieving the ball, Otis bounded back towards the living room. Emma continued to play with him for several minutes, tossing the ball back into the kitchen. Obviously, this was a game they had played many times before. Once the game was over, he heard Emma say "Let's head for bed, okay?"

Jake switched to the camera in the ceiling fan, so could see her on the monitor as she came up the stairs. Emma went straight into the bathroom, and a few seconds later he heard the sound of water running. She walked back out into the hall, entering her bedroom. Soft instrumental music of old movie love songs filled the upstairs of the house. While listening to her move about, Jake closed his eyes, letting his imagination wander. In his mind, he could see her preparing her bath, and then submerging herself in layers of bubbles. Remembering the forest-like atmosphere that she had created around the Jacuzzi, he saw himself with her in that luxurious oversized tub. Jake started to create a detailed image of her. She would have a petite, but strong, well proportioned body. Her breasts would be firm and perky, and her buttock small and round. Her arms and legs would be well muscled and athletic. A perfect picture in his mind.

Upon opening his eyes, he discovered that perfect picture was now right there in front of him. The image in his mind had transferred itself to the monitor screen, almost as if he had willed it to life. Emma was standing naked in the bedroom door, wine glass in hand. For some reason, it had never crossed Jake's mind, when planting the camera in the hall, that this would happen, although it should have. After all, she did live out in the country by herself, and with her window shades drawn, was probably unconcerned about anyone seeing her. Even though he was positive that she didn't know the camera existed, he was still startled when, with an uncanny awareness, she titled her head up and smiled at him. He held his breath as her beautiful face continued to look at him from the screen. Slowly she looked away, and walked toward the bathroom.

Emma was humming along softly to the music on the CD, as she shut off the water. There was a slight clicking sound coming from the hallway. Looking at the monitor, he watched as Otis made his way out of the bedroom and into the bathroom, his nails tapping against the hardwood floors.

"Well, what do you think, Oats? Is it time for me to start looking for a man again?" Emma's voice drifted into the cabin. "You like Matt, don't you? I think he's charming and pretty cute. Tomorrow should be a lot of fun. And, who knows where it'll go from there."

Jake could feel every fiber of his body tense with jealousy. His stomach felt like someone had just punched him, and he could feel himself becoming upset with Emma for talking that way. Logic told him he was being ridiculous, but he couldn't seem to help himself. Hell, she didn't even know he existed. Well, that wasn't quite true, she knew he existed, she just didn't know who he was. Even so, Jake didn't like hearing her refer to the Deputy that way. He tried to remind himself to stay professional and remain in control, that he had been hired to do a job, even if it was becoming impossible to do so.

"You know though, before I jump into anything, I think I'd like to meet this friend of yours." Emma said to the dog, who answered her with a soft huff. "He's kind of secretive, but, after today I almost feel compelled to find out who he is." At the sound of her words, Jake's body started to relax. Maybe he had a chance with her after all. He continued to monitor her until he was sure that she was safe and asleep in bed, and then went to bed himself. However, his sleep was fitful as his mind tried to find a way out of the ethical dilemma he had gotten himself into.

Saturday morning turned out to be beautiful. The bright blue sky had been washed clean by the rainstorm that had thundered its way through the Ozarks the night before. Jake poured himself a cup of coffee and stepped out on the porch. The musty smell of damp earth filled the morning air, and left over drops of rain sparkled like small diamonds as they fell off the leaves of the giant oak trees. He knew Emma would be sitting on her porch, enjoying her coffee about now. Wrestling most of the night with what he really wanted to do, and knowing if he wanted to contact her, he concluded that there was only one choice. Leaving the door open, Jake walked back in and sat at the kitchen table in front of his computer. Logging on, he went to his e-mail, and clicked on the address book. He selected the e-mail address for his anonymous client.

> *I need to let you know that I can no longer be involved in this case the way you requested. I feel that the danger to Ms. Hudson is increasing on a daily basis, and it is becoming difficult to protect her from a distance. I have decided to speak*

*with her, and inform her of the situation. I am aware that you
believe this will put her in further harm, and have requested
that I not do this. However, I disagree with your assessment of
the situation. So, as of today, I am terminating my services
with you. However, please rest assured that Ms. Hudson will
be protected until I feel she is out of danger.*

*Jake McLean*

Jake reread the message, his finger on the mouse as the arrow
hovered over the "Send" button. He could only hope and pray
that what he was about to do was for Emma's good, and not just
some raging hormones taking over his rational thinking. Was he
foolish not to heed his client's warning? Should he give his client
a little more time to obtain the needed information? While Jake's
mind questioned his motives and judgment, gut instinct told him
he was right, and Jake trusted his gut. He had ignored that instinct
only once before, with disastrous results. Flashing back, he could
see Laura Campbell, playing and laughing with her daughter, but,
those pictures were quickly replaced by ones of a bullet ridden,
handless body, and blood soaked room. Jake shut his eyes tight
against the images that flooded his memory. He would never let
that happen again. He clicked the mouse. The message "Your
Mail Has Been Sent" appeared on his screen.

\* \* \*

Emma loved thunderstorms. Last night, while relaxing with
her wine in the tub, she had watched the white hot flashes of
lightning as they danced across the sky. A number of times the
explosion of the thunder was so close it rocked the old farmhouse
from top to bottom. Since she was a child, Emma had been
fascinated by thunder and lightning storms. As she grew older,

common sense told her that storms like these could become violent, resulting in floods and, sometimes, tornados. The child in her, however, tended to overrule this adult logic, seeing the storms only as something magical and mysterious. She had fallen asleep to the sound of rain drumming on the roof, and the squeak of tree limbs rubbing up along the side of the house.

Emma had awakened this morning filled with excitement. It had been a long time since she had dated, and she felt like a school girl getting ready for the prom. She spent the morning trying on outfit after outfit, wanting to make sure that the one she picked would be just right. Otis was sprawled out on her bed, yawning, as Emma modeled every outfit for him. Trying on everything from tailor-made suits to simple jeans and a sweater, she decided on a seafoam green dress with lavender flowers. The dress was simple with thin straps, a scooped neckline, and a flowing skirt that ended in gentle waves about mid-calf. The soft fabric and princess style design hugged the curves of her body, showing off every feminine feature she had. As with the dress, Emma had tried a number of hair styles, but, ended up leaving her chestnut hair in the silky natural curls that suited her so well. A comb of small violets in her hair, and a simple diamond pendant around her neck, accented her outfit.

Emma had had an overpowering need today to look her best. Her conscience mind led her to believe it was because it was her first date in many years with a charming, handsome man. But her subconscious mind hinted that tonight would not be as Emma expected, and she would want to look beautiful for "him". Making one more full turn in the mirror, she had to admit she did feel beautiful.

Walking toward the head of the stairs, the hair on Emma's neck began to tingle. She stopped in the middle of the hall, searching for the source of the electrical current that seemed to be in the air. Last night, she had had the same feeling, almost like someone was watching her. Nothing seemed out of place, and yet she felt nervous. Emma thought about the presence that had been in the woods the night before last, but this wasn't the same. She had been scared then, and Otis had been extremely upset. Maybe she was just imagining things, as the dog seemed totally oblivious to not only any unnamed phenomenon that might be lurking in the house, but, to her own anxiety. She looked down at him, shaking her head.

"Some watch dog you are." Choosing to ignore her, Otis padded on by and headed down the stairs. Emma went to the kitchen to tidy things up before Matt's arrival. Glancing out the window above the sink, she saw Matt's pickup coming down the drive. Putting the last of the dishes away, she turned towards the back door to lock up. That same feeling from upstairs hit her again, and she spun around expecting to see someone standing in the doorway. Of course, no one was there. Her eyes inspected every corner of the big kitchen, as she locked the door and walked slowly toward the living room.

"I must be going crazy." She was talking to herself, as much as she was the dog. "First I'm seeing a man appear in the woods, then one disappears in broad daylight, and now I think I have ghosts watching me in my own house. Maybe what I need is a *"ghostbuster"*. Think I'll call Bill Murray when we get home." The dog shook his head, and gave her a look that said he thought she might be just a little bit crazy.

Opening the front door, Emma stepped out on the porch, with Otis bounding out ahead of her. She double checked the locks on the door, then watched Matt lower the tailgate of his truck, allowing Otis to jump in the back.

"Deputy Green, are you really taking that mutt with you?" Emma asked.

"Thought with it bein' our first date and all, perhaps we should have a chaperone. This one shouldn't give us too much trouble." Matt said, scratching the big dog's ears.

"Don't be too sure about that. He's got quite a mind of his own, and he's not opposed to forcing his opinion upon you." Emma warned him.

"I think I'll take my chances." Matt grinned. "Boy, you sure look beautiful today." Walking toward her, Emma saw the appreciative expression on his face that told her all her fussing from the morning had paid off.

"Why, thank you, sir."

"So, are you ready to go?"

"Yeah." Emma smiled, and Matt offered her his hand, leading her down the steps and over to his truck.

\* \* \*

Jake had watched and listened to her this morning as she had gone through the rituals of first date impressions. He wished, however, it had been for him that she had spent so much time making everything perfect. Earlier today, he'd been a little concerned that maybe she was aware he was watching her. Twice she'd looked directly where he had positioned the cameras. Emma hadn't seemed scared, but her expression left no doubt she was suspicious that there was something different about her house. Through the images coming from the perimeter cameras, he watched her drive off with the Deputy towards town. Now it was his turn to get ready for their first date.

# Chapter Eleven

The festivities were in full swing by the time Matt and Emma arrived in town. Along with the residents of Cedar Falls, and the locals from the surrounding countryside, the Annual Fall Festival attracted many visitors. Some were looking for good deals on the wares being sold, but, many were just enjoying the atmosphere of a small town celebration, much as Emma was doing. The square was full of craftsmen selling everything from homemade jellies and jams to quilts and handmade furniture. There were various carnival games, at which both children and adults alike were having a grand time trying their skills for prizes, but, mostly losing their money. The air was full of the wonderful smell of grilled hot dogs and hamburgers, Bar-B-Que, and potatoes with onions that were being fried in big cast onion skillets that looked more like giant woks. The dance floor was finished, and decorated with paper lanterns strung along the wires from one tall corner post to the other. Country and bluegrass musicians were entertaining the crowds from the gazebo.

Matt and Emma took their time strolling between the tables and booths, examining the exquisite craftsmanship of the items that were for sale. The intricate carvings of the woodworker fascinated her, as did the delicate stitching that was involved in the making of quilts. A potter, who had set up his wheel, was giving demonstrations of the skill it took to mold beautiful dishes and vases out of a simple lump of brownish-grey clay. Also performing his craft was a basket weaver, who was producing baskets of various shapes, colors, and sizes, from strips of dried wood. At one of the woodworker's booths, Emma purchased a small, wooden jewelry box, with roses inlaid in mother-of-pearl on the top. Next, they wandered over to the games, all of whose proceeds were to go to the county library for new books. Both tried their skill at the ring toss, to no avail, and didn't fair much better at "tossing the baseball into the milk can" game. However, the shooting gallery was next in line.

"You think I have a chance of winning this one?" Matt asked Emma.

"I certainly hope so, otherwise, I'm going to have to check out just where you went to deputy school," she teased.

Aiming the small rifle, Matt picked off five little ducks in a row with ease.

"I should have put up a sign 'For Amateur's Only'," grumbled Ralph Daley, as he took the rifle back from Matt. "Between you, Sheriff Henderson, and Peter O'Hara, I'll be out of prizes before the afternoon's half over."

"Well, maybe you should limit us 'professionals' to one turn only," Matt laughed. "Now, what's my prize?"

"You can have either the stuffed bear, or the outer space laser gun."

"Well, of course, my preference would be the bear, but I'll ask the lady what she thinks."

"Oh, I kind of like the laser gun, but it doesn't really go with my decor." Emma quipped. "I think the bear would look better on my bed."

Ralph chuckled, handing Emma the bear and giving her a wink. They continued down the aisle checking out the other games available to take their money. Emma felt a tug on the bear's leg, as the fluffy stuffed animal was pulled from her grasp. Quickly bending over, she was able to catch a hold of it just before it hit the dirt, coming nose to nose with Otis.

"Just what do you think you're doing?" she whispered between clenched teeth at the dog. Unfazed by the harsh tone of her voice, Otis nudged the bear with his nose, trying again to dislodge it from her hands.

Matt reached down offering her his hand. "It appears that this canine wants to abscond with your bear."

Emma stood up, keeping the bear securely out of Otis' reach. "He's just jealous because he doesn't have one of his own. He's got this "what's yours is mine, and what's mine is mine" kind of attitude, you know?"

"Well, we may just have to try to win him somethin' then."

"I warned you about bringing him. Didn't I say he had a mind of his own?"

"Yeah, you're right, you did warn me, but he wants to have fun, too. Just look at him."

They both looked down at the dog, who was giving them his best sad, puppy dog face. However, the mischievous twinkle in his eye made Emma quite aware that he knew exactly what he was doing. Matt looked around and, seeing that no one was playing the basketball toss, led the three of them over to that booth. Neither Matt nor Emma noticed as something further down the aisle caught Otis' attention, and he wandered off. They both took a turn shooting the baskets with Emma getting two out of five, and Matt making three baskets. Emma's prize was a necklace with a small, gold plated heart on it, and Matt won a Frisbee.

"Well, it's not a stuffed animal, but we can have some fun

throwin' it around, don't ya think?" Matt asked, a small hint of disappointment in his voice.

"Trust me, he'll love it." Emma gave him a reassuring smile. "Just be prepared that anytime you come over though, he'll be wanting you to play with him, and he can go on forever chasing things."

"That shouldn't be too hard, I've got a lot of stamina." Matt laughed, feeling better about the prize he had won. "By the way, where'd he go?"

They looked around, not seeing the dog anywhere in sight. Emma let out an exasperated sigh. He could be so annoying sometimes. They started checking out a number of the other booths that lined the midway. She was just about to call out the dog's name when Emma spotted him leaving the dart booth, prancing towards her with something in his mouth.

"There he is," she said, leading Matt in the direction of the dog. As they got closer, she noticed whatever was in Otis' mouth was bright orange and black. Emma kneeled down as he came up to her, displaying with pride his newest possession.

"Let me see what you have," Emma said. Otis eyed her with suspicion, not wanting to give up his hard won prize. "Drop it, right now." The object he laid, with some reluctance, at her feet turned out to be a stuffed tiger.

"Looks like he got himself a stuff animal after all." Matt chuckled as he knelt down beside her.

"Where did you get this? You know better than that." Emma scolded the dog, who sat still, looking longingly at the tiger. Embarrassed, she turned to Matt, saying, "Can you believe it, I'm on a date with a Deputy Sheriff, and I've got a thief for a dog."

Matt grinned at her. "I wouldn't worry too much. From the value of the merchandise, I'd say he only committed a misdemeanor."

Appreciating Matt's effort to make light of the situation, she still knew she had to return the tiger. Keeping the stuffed animal in her hand, she stood up and headed for the dart booth, Otis trotting at her heels. Sara Morgan, a cute, bubbly, blonde, who was also the high school homecoming queen, was operating the booth. She had witnessed Emma's reprimand of the dog, and had already prepared herself for Emma's arrival.

"I see that Otis showed you his prize," Sara said, referring to the tiger in Emma's arms.

"Oh, Sara, I'm so embarrassed," Emma apologized. "I can't believe that he took this right in front of you. He's usually really good about not taking things that aren't his. I don't know what got into him."

"But, Emma, it is his. He didn't steal it, did you, Otis?" Sara smiled as she reached over the counter, petting the big dog's head. He licked her hand in return, grateful for her support.

Surprised, Emma looked from the dog, to Matt, and back to Sara. "What do you mean it's his?"

"Some guy was shooting darts," Sara explained. "Hit five out of five, so he won the tiger. Otis was standin' there, and this guy gave it to him."

"Who was he? Why would he do that?"

"I don't know who he was, but I'm pretty sure Otis did. He came right over when the guy called him by name." Leaning toward Emma, Sara whispered in her ear, "And, what's more, he was quite a hunk. As far as I'm concerned, he could've stayed at my booth all day."

Emma looked at Matt, a completely baffled look on her face.

"I guess Otis has friends you don't know about, huh?"

"Yeah, I guess so," Emma replied, shrugging her shoulders.

"Well, don't let it bother you too much. You know how kids are these days, they never let you know what they're doin'."

She wasn't about to tell Matt that she had a pretty good idea who Otis' friend was.

"So, are you ready to eat?" Matt asked. "The dinner tent should be open about now. Thought we might wander over that direction."

"Actually, I am getting rather hungry. All this food smells so wonderful."

"How about I take our winnings back to the truck? Free up our hands for important things like fried chicken." Taking Emma's bear, and packages from her, along with the tiger, Matt headed for the street. Maneuvering himself in front of Matt, Otis planted himself down in front of the Deputy's feet, blocking his way. Letting out a soft bark, he stared at the tiger in Matt's hand. Matt looked down at the big retriever. "You're going to have to ask your mom first."

"Can you believe how spoiled he is?" Emma said. "Go ahead and give him the tiger back. I don't know how he plans to eat though."

"Right now, I don't think he cares about eating." Matt handed the dog back his stuffed animal.

"How about I meet you back over by the quilts? There was one there I wanted to take a look at again."

"I'll be there in just a few."

Arms full, Matt headed off in the direction where they had parked his truck. Emma worked her way through the crowds, greeting many of her friends, winding up at the quilting booth. Earlier, she had been looking at a beautiful wedding ring quilt, done in lovely shades of pale blue, lavender and green. She had been wanting an original, handmade quilt for her bedroom since she had moved here, and had now found one with the right colors. Walking over to the spot where the quilt had been hanging earlier in the day, disappointment set in when she didn't see it. In the midst of the forest of colorful fabrics and designs, sat an older woman who was working on a new quilt. Her fingers, gnarled with arthritis, still sewed each tiny stitch that held the different patterns and colors together with skill and precision. Emma watched her for a few moments, marveling at her handiwork.

"Excuse me." The old woman raised her head. Emma was taken back by the old woman's penetrating eyes which, in contrast to the silver hair that hung in a braid down her back, appeared to be almost black. Despite the wrinkles that came with someone her age, the old woman's face was soft rather than leathery. Crow's feet around her eyes deepened as she gave Emma a warm, pleasant smile.

Finding her voice again, Emma asked, "There was a green and lavender wedding ring quilt here earlier today. Do you still have it?"

"Oh, I remember you," the woman said. "You spent quite a while looking at that quilt. I was sure you were gonna buy it."

"Do you still have it?"

"I'm sorry, dear, but I sold it not long after you left. It really was a lovely quilt."

Emma was disgusted with herself. It seemed that she always had to wrestle back and forth with her conscience before buying something new. Emma knew she created this habit in herself because her father had always told her to make double sure she wanted something before spending her money on it, however, she was pretty sure her father hadn't intended for her to take it to the extreme she did sometimes. Now her procrastination had once more caused her to lose out on something she had been wanting for a long time and had now found. Dejected, she sat in the chair next to the old woman. Otis, who had already managed to introduced himself to her, had his head in the woman's lap.

"Is there any chance that you could make another one like it?"

Emma asked. "I loved both the colors and design, they were perfect for my bedroom."

Sitting back, the old woman said thoughtfully, "I never make two quilts the same, but I could make you somethin' similar, with those same kind of colors, if you'd like."

"Oh, that would be wonderful," Emma said, laying her hand on the other woman's, giving it a pat.

At Emma's touch, the old woman immediately trapped Emma's hand between her own. The strength of those arthritic ridden hands surprised Emma. The woman's facial expression had become serious, and her dark eyes searched Emma's own soft, green ones. Wanting to look away, Emma found she couldn't. To anyone observing the two of them, it would appear that they were having nothing more than an in-depth conversation. However, as Emma continued to be lost in the those hypnotic eyes, it was as if the old woman was not just looking at her, but was reaching deep into her soul. Within a few short minutes, the old woman's eyes focused again on Emma's face, and she spoke almost in a whisper.

"There are two powerful, opposing forces trying to enter your life. One is full of warmth and light, and is trying to protect you, to keep you safe. But, there is another darker, evil force that is of great danger to you. Tonight will be a night of confusion and conflict for you. Your mind will tell you one thing, and your heart another." With one more intense look into Emma's eyes, she said, "Always trust in your heart."

Releasing Emma's hand, the old woman stroked Otis' head, which hadn't moved once during the preceding exchange. Even though she was still shaken, Emma couldn't help but notice the similarity in color between the old woman's eyes and the dog's. The feeling she had just experienced with the old woman had been familiar. She knew, now, it was the same feeling she had felt on a number of occasions when Otis acted as if he read her mind.

"He's a wonderful dog." Caressing Otis' broad head, the old woman continued, "However, I think you already know he's more than just a dog, he's your guardian. His heart is true and faithful, he'll always lead you home. In what is to come, you may doubt yourself, but, do not doubt him."

Emma was about to ask the old woman to clarify what it was that she should be watching out for, what the danger was that lay ahead, when a hand grasped her shoulder. Startled, she turned so quick that she barely missed stabbing Matt in the ribs with her elbow.

"Are you okay?" Matt noticed right away how pale Emma's face was. "You look like you've seen a ghost."

"Uh…, yeah…, I'm all right," Emma stammered. "Let's go get something to eat."

Emma linked her arm through Matt's, attempting to turn him away from the quilting booth. However, Matt remained solid, right where he was.

"How's everything goin', Martha?" The quiet inflection in Matt's voice let Martha Quinn know he was aware of the type of conversation she had just had with Emma. Martha knew that Matt was not as suspicious of her "special gift" as the other locals where, but, she also knew that he would rather she kept things to herself. She gave Matt an innocent look.

"Why, everythin's fine, Matthew, thank you for askin'. And, yourself?"

"I'm fine. I see you've found yourself a friend." Matt said, nodding at Otis who had yet to leave the old woman's side.

"Oh, yes, he's quite remarkable. We think a lot alike. He's told me quite a lot." The old woman ran her crooked fingers one more time through the soft fur of Otis' neck before he decided to raise his head and walk over to Emma.

"He has, has he. Well, I hope it was mostly good."

"Mostly."

"Well, you have a nice evenin', Martha." Matt turned toward Emma, reaching for her hand.

"Matthew," the tone of the old woman's voice caused him to turn back around. She gave him a knowing smile. "Don't be too disappointed. Whatever happens to us in our life is by God's hand, and is meant to be."

Looking a bit confused, Matt just said, "I'll try to remember that, Martha."

# Chapter Twelve

Matt took Emma's hand and led her toward the large red and white stripped tent where the evening's fried chicken dinner was being served. Neither of them said anything as they took their place in line. Showing good manners, Otis laid down just outside the tent door, his tiger tucked safely between his paws. Wonderful aromas filled the air, and Emma's stomach grumbled, as she realized she hadn't eaten since breakfast. The servers piled their plates high with fried chicken, mashed potatoes and gravy, green beans, okra (which Emma politely declined), biscuits, and either cherry cobbler or pumpkin pie for dessert. Even after almost a year of living here, Emma still couldn't seem to get use to how much everyone ate. To the "high society" people she had known in Denver, a big dinner would have consisted of a large chef's salad.

Finding a table near the entrance of the tent where Otis had stationed himself, they were about to sit down when Emma noticed a head of silver hair bobbing and weaving its way through the crowd. Whispering something in Matt's ear, she set her plate down and made a beeline for Henry. Coming up behind him, she tapped him on the shoulder.

"Hey, boss, how about joining Matt and me for dinner?"

At the sound of Emma's voice, Henry turned around, a smile lighting up his face. Looking over Henry's shoulder, Emma noticed a woman who had also stopped and turned around. Emma guessed her to be Henry's new love. For some reason, Emma had imagined that she would be tall, sophisticated, and elegant, but, this delightful looking woman was just the opposite. She was short and slightly plump. Her salt and pepper hair was styled in close curls on her head, and she had gentle brown eyes like those of a fawn. The soft, red sweater she wore set off the fine olive complexion of her skin.

"Emma, I'd like you to meet Angela Castrone. She has graciously consented to be my companion today." Henry said, moving aside so that Angela could step up next to him.

"I'm very happy to meet you," Angela said with a bright smile. "Henry has told me so much about you."

"Oh, has he now. Well, he hasn't told me a thing about you," Emma replied, crossing her arms, and raising her eyebrows at Henry. "I pretty much figured out he had someone special in his life though, because every time he returned from Springfield, his feet never touched the ground for days. You seem to have quite an effect on this ornery, old attorney." Emma winked at Angela, as a rosy pink crept its way up Henry's face.

"Well, that's Henry," Angela jested, "Must be a lawyer thing, confidentiality and all, you know."

Emma laughed and gave Henry a quick hug, as the old man continued to blush.

Looking for a way out of his predicament, he asked Emma, "Do you have room for two at your table?"

"Why, of course. We're over this way." Emma led them back through the sea of red and white checked table cloths to the table where Matt was waiting.

After formal introductions were made, they all settled back to enjoy the tasty meal, and good conversation. Emma liked Angela right away, knowing she would be good for Henry. She had been the judge's secretary for the past 20 years, so she and Henry had a lot in common. With everyone at the table being in some kind of legal profession, the conversation naturally turned into an exchange of stories about various cases each one had worked. Henry was in the middle of telling about an unsolved murder case from 10 years ago, when a tingle of the electrical current Emma had felt that morning started up her spine. Whipping her head around, her eyes searched the tent for something, anything, that might be causing this sensation. She thought she had left the ghosts at home, but her senses told her she was being watched.

"Emma, are you all right?" Henry asked, concern tinting his voice, "You're as white as a sheet."

"She looked this way earlier, after spending a little time with Martha Quinn this afternoon," Matt said, giving Henry a knowing look.

"Oh, I see." Henry sat back in his chair, nodding. "And, what did our own dear Martha have to tell you, Emma?"

"Nothing, really." Emma said, staring down at her half-eaten dinner.

"She must have said something to have upset you so."

"No. Not anything specific anyway. Just something about good and evil forces coming into my life, and that I should trust my heart." Emma continued to stare at her plate, making small designs in the mashed potatoes with her fork.

"Well, that's kind of vague," Henry spoke to her in a fatherly tone. "Emma, I've known Martha a long time. She likes to have people think that she can see into the future. But, when you think about it, don't all of us grapple with good and evil in our lives every day? And, it's only common sense to trust in your heart."

"I suppose so. But, she also told me not to ever doubt Otis."

Both Matt and Henry broke out in laughter. "She claims that she can talk with the animals. Read their minds and such," Matt said. "As far as Otis is concerned, I don't think he'd ever let you doubt him. He's got a mind of his own, remember?"

"I know you're right. She just seemed so sure is all." Emma gave them a look that seemed to put them at ease. However, in the back of her mind, she knew she would always heed the old woman's warning.

Finishing their dinner, they shifted the course of the conversation to what most people refer to as "chitchat". Matt and Henry reminisced about how Cedar Falls used to be, and the changes that had taken place over the years. They filled Angela in on the town gossip, pointing out various people and giving, what was sometimes quite colorful, descriptions of their lives. Emma had heard a number of the stories before, but, even some were new to her, and she enjoyed the feeling of becoming a part of the community. As evening fell, they heard the band in the gazebo start playing, and the paper lanterns around the dance floor sprang to life. In silent agreement, they all left the table and wandered out of the tent to enjoy the evening air. The music drifted on the breeze, weaving its way in and around the trees, filling up the little park. The various vendors started closing down their booths, coming over to join in the night's activities.

The next hour was filled with socializing and dancing. Matt and Emma visited with a number of their friends, and helped Henry introduce Angela around. They also took a number of spins around the floor, dancing the two-step and jitterbug. Matt was a good dancer and seemed to be enjoying himself, however, Emma noticed that when the music became soft and the dancing slow, Matt wouldn't ask her to dance. All Emma could figure was, being their first date and knowing Matt could be somewhat shy, perhaps he was a little unsure of being that physically close. Emma smiled to herself. What she remembered of dating was if the guy could get you in the back seat of his car on the first date he would. She wasn't even close to being ready for that, though she wouldn't have minded a slow dance or two.

Emma was having fun observing all the different people, when her eyes came to rest on a stunning woman standing across the dance floor. It took her a minute to realize it was Maggie O'Hara. Wearing a deep purple dress that complemented, not only her impressive figure, but her lovely lavender eyes, Maggie looked amazing. Her auburn hair, which she wore in a French roll while working, now hung in loose waves around her bare shoulders. She was standing with Sara Morgan, who seemed to be telling Maggie something of great importance. The two leaned closer together in what appeared to be almost a conspiratorial manner, then laughed as they both looked around the park, as if searching for someone.

"So, would you care to dance again?" Matt asked Emma.

Evading his question, Emma said, "Have you seen Maggie? She really looks beautiful tonight."

"I'm sure she does, but she can't look as good as you do."

"Well, I appreciate that," she said, flashing Matt a sly smile, "But I don't think Maggie has been out on the dance floor yet, and somebody should show her off."

Matt gave her an over exaggerated look of shock. "Are you pushin' me into the arms of another woman?"

"Of course not," Emma laughed, "But I do think someone should ask her to dance, and you're such a fine dancer. So, how about it?"

"You don't have to butter me up, Emma. Especially when you're wrong. However, I'll do it for you."

"Thank you very much. You're quite the gentleman."

Matt smiled, "Okay, so where is she?"

"Right across the dance floor."

Matt scanned the crowd at the edge of the platform. "Where?"

"Right there." Emma pointed a finger at where Maggie was standing.

"That's Maggie!" Matt exclaimed, obvious disbelief on his face.

"Didn't I tell you she looked beautiful?"

"Wow, she looks great! Quite a change from the café."

The stunned look on Matt's face actually caused a small prick of jealousy in Emma. However, she quickly dispelled it, encouraging Matt, and sending him on his way. She liked Matt, a lot, but, she wasn't sure she was ready for any type of commitment. Besides, deep down she knew that he belonged with Maggie. Emma was watching Matt and Maggie step out onto the floor, when a blast of icy air came out of nowhere, slithering its way up her back. Like before, she felt as if someone was watching her, but it wasn't the same feeling she had had at the house. This air around her was cold and menacing. Emma's ears caught the sound of a low, rumbling growl coming from Otis. He was looking behind her, reacting as he had a few nights ago. Remembering the old woman's words, she turned around. Panic almost seized her as, in desperation, she tried to survey the crowd through the darkness for some sign of what might be out there. Then, just as quick as it had appeared, the coldness left, and a soft, warm breeze surrounded her. The hair on the back of Otis' head was now lying flat against his sleek neck, his ears pricked forward. Telling herself she was foolish, she turned around without looking where she was going, and ran smack into a wall of solid muscle.

Emma looked up, intending to apologize to the unfortunate person she had run into, and found herself staring into the most mesmerizing eyes she had ever seen. Thick, dark lashes surrounded the unique silver-grey eyes which, in one split second, had captured her own. She tried to bring the rest of his face into focus, but couldn't tear her eyes away from his. In the background, Emma heard the band strike up a waltz. Waltzes had always been her favorite. She loved the feeling of moving around the dance floor in three-quarters time, to music which made you feel as if you were floating on the clouds. As if reading her mind, and without asking her permission, he seized her hand and swept her onto the dance floor.

He was tall and strong. Emma could feel the strength in the arm which encircled her waist, holding her tightly against him. Her free hand had found its way up to his shoulder and, seeming to have a mind of its own, began to roam. Through his shirt, she could feel the solidness of his muscles. Tracing the contours of his shoulders, upper back and arm, it surprised her how his muscles tensed under the touch of her fingers. Emma looked up to find him studying her. She was sure that he sensed her embarrassment at having so boldly explored his body, without so much as an introduction. The waltz started to end, and she realized that it felt like her feet had never touched the floor, as if he simply picked her up and carried her throughout the entire dance. By the time reality set back in, he had already led her off the side of the platform, away from the crowd, toward a grouping of giant oak trees. The words "good" and "evil" played against each other in her mind, and she wondered what she was doing following him without so much as a moments hesitation.

Stopping at the base of the trees, he turned towards her and leaned up against the trunk. The light from the dance floor tried to filter its way through the branches above them. Emma concentrated on his face, which was half hidden, not only by the shadows, but by the thick, dark hair that flowed along his face and neck. He had a broad forehead and a straight, almost aristocratic nose. A small scar ran along the edge of his high set cheekbone. Emma's eyes shifted to his jaw which was strong and square, and then settled in on his mouth. She marveled at the sensuality of his lips, while the tip of her tongue traced the outline of her own.

"You're the one who's been watching me," Emma stated, making eye contact with him.

"I'm one of 'em," Jake answered.

"The good one, I hope," Emma said, looking back over her shoulder.

Jake hadn't been certain whether Emma had been aware of the other presence. He knew the dog had, but now he knew she did, too.

"Yeah, I'm the good one, and I need to talk to you, but not here." Pushing himself away from the tree, Jake reached for Emma's hand, intending to lead her to his truck.

Emma snatched her hand back. "I'm not going anywhere with you. First of all, I don't even know your name, and, second, I have no idea why you're watching me. Why in the world would I just go off with you?"

"Okay. First, my name's Jake McLean. Second, I'm a private investigator who was hired to watch you. And, you need to go with me so I can fill you in on all the details. I don't want to do it here, so let's go."

As Jake reached for her again, Emma took a couple of steps backwards to avoid his grasp, stumbling over Otis who had appeared out of the darkness. Jake's arm snaked around her waist, stopping her before she hit the ground. With little effort, he lifted her up and set her on her feet.

"Well, look who's here. Are you enjoying the tiger?" Jake knelt down and the dog bounded over to greet him, still clutching his new toy. Otis' tail was spinning so fast in a circle that he reminded

Emma of those old fashioned rubber band toys that you wind up and then let go flying across the table top.

Emma looked down at Jake, who was scratching Otis' chest. "He sure has taken a liking to you."

"He's a good judge of character."

"I always thought so." A hint of reservation was in Emma's voice.

"You think he made a mistake this time?" Jake's face showed no emotion, it was just a simple question.

"I don't know. I don't think so," Emma said, still not sounding completely convinced. "Don't doubt the dog," She mumbled under her breath.

"What'd you say?"

"Nothing. Look...Mr. McLean, is it? Anyway, if you want to talk to me it will have to be later."

Giving Otis a final pat, Jake stood up and looked down at Emma. She could see the seriousness of the expression on his face.

"I think we should talk now. I can drive you home, and we can discuss it on the way."

"I don't know who you think you are, Mr. McLean," Emma said, irritation seeping into her voice, "but, I'm here on a date, and I don't intend to skip out on him. If you wish to come by tomorrow, I'll see you then. Right now, I'm going back to the dance."

Jake wanted to make sure that Emma got home safe. He knew the other presence had been around all day watching her. However, he also bristled at the reminder that she was here with the deputy. Selfishly, Jake wanted to make sure that this date of her's ended up as platonic as it started out. He could accomplish both objectives if he could get her to go with him now.

Grabbing her, he said, "That's not good enough. I want...no,

I need to talk to you tonight." The feeling of his fingers tightening around her upper arms made Emma even more determined to resist him. Pushing against his chest with her hands, she broke free from his grasp.

"Well, it'll have to be good enough. Now, I'm going back to my friends, and I'll see you tomorrow." She started back toward the lights of the festival.

"I'll see you before that." The hard, self-assured tone of his voice made Emma turn back around.

"Is that a threat?"

"No. More like a promise."

Looking him eye to eye, she said defiantly, "I'm not scared of you, Mr. McLean!"

He stepped forward, closing the distance between them to just a few inches. The moonlight made his silver eyes glint like polished steel, and in a voice so soft and low it almost made her heart stop, he said, "Maybe you should be, Ms. Hudson."

# Chapter Thirteen

The eyes had observed the exchange that was taking place by the oak trees. Emma had watched Jake until he faded into the darkness at the edge of the park. Now they followed her as she returned to where her friends were. The deputy's face showed concern as he spoke to her. She shook her head, giving him a false smile. He must have felt her anxiety though because he protectively put his arm around her, and his eyes scanned the park for anything suspicious.

The eyes had watched Emma for most of the day. With a few minor changes to the appearance of the body that they resided in, they now looked quite ordinary and unmemorable. Not overly good looking, not ugly, just basically nondescript. A person could blend into a crowd so easily that way. Neither Emma, the investigator, nor the deputy had noticed them. Only once today had they even suspected that someone knew they were there. They'd been observing Emma in an intense conversation with an old woman, when all of sudden they were sure that the old woman was aware of them. It didn't matter that she never once looked in their direction, she knew they were there. The feeling had been unsettling, however, it was soon forgotten as there were more important things to think about.

While watching Emma now, laughing and enjoying herself, they thought how quickly she had become comfortable in this community. Much more so than she ever was in the high society circles her husband had traveled in in Denver. They'd always known she never really fit in there, even if Charles couldn't see it. She'd tried her best, but was never truly happy. Now she was, and they should've been glad for her, but, they weren't. They were becoming ever more jealous with each passing day, particularly of the men in her life. Though the increased surveillance, and attention, of the investigator was becoming frustrating, they realized he had been hired to do a job. The continued interference of the deputy, however, was another story, and was causing a rage to start building within.

The eyes focused on Emma who was again on the dance floor securely embraced in the deputy's arms. They were dancing their first slow dance of the evening, swaying to the familiar strains of some old fifties song. Glancing away, the eyes tried to calm the rage that had just increased another degree in their brain. For the plan to work they had to think clearly. However, like an unstable pressure cooker, they knew an explosion was coming that couldn't be stopped.

# Chapter Fourteen

Jake was angry. Angry with her, and angry with himself. How could he warn her if she wouldn't listen to him. A little, nagging voice in the back of his mind reminded him that tonight had been more his fault than Emma's. She'd been having a good time dining and dancing with her friends, seeming oblivious to the danger surrounding her. He'd waited well into the evening for the precise opportunity to reveal himself. When the deputy had left her side to dance with the sexy redhead, Jake had moved in. He'd meant to be professional, intending to introduce himself and to ask her to sit down and hear him out. All those good intentions changed when she ran into him. Jake had looked down into the depths of those sea green eyes, and all his better instincts disappeared. Without uttering a single word to her, he'd had swept her away onto the dance floor. She hadn't resisted him when he pulled her close enough to him that her breasts brushed up against his chest. Even through his shirt, Jake's skin had felt on fire when Emma explored his body with her fingertips. She'd felt small and fragile in his arms, and that feeling had overwhelmed him with a wave of possessiveness toward her. That's probably why he was so upset with her for not leaving with him. Logic told him that he should have expected her to be cautious, but, having been that close to her his logic had taken a back seat to his emotions. So, now, he could do nothing but wait.

It was a little after two o'clock in the morning when Jake heard the deputy's truck pull up. He'd drifted in and out of a fitful sleep waiting for her to come home. The sound of their footsteps reached his ears as Matt walked Emma to the front door. Remaining still in the shadows, he eavesdropped on their conversation.

"Thanks for a wonderful day." Emma said. "I had a lot of fun."

"So, did I. Maybe we can do it again sometime. Go to a movie, or somethin'."

"I'd like that. And, maybe, we could leave the chaperone at home next time." They both grinned at the insulted look that Otis gave them. "I swear that he knows exactly what I'm saying sometimes."

"Well, accordin' to Martha Quinn, he does." Matt started to chuckle, but stopped as a frown appeared on Emma's face. "Emma, you're not lettin' what Martha said get to ya, are ya?"

"I know I shouldn't, but, I can't help thinking about it. I wasn't going to tell you until I was certain, but I'm pretty sure someone has been watching me."

Jake's body froze. Had he blown it earlier? He couldn't believe she was going to tell the deputy about him. After the way she'd looked at him tonight, he'd been positive she was going to give him a chance to explain everything.

"Do you have any idea who it is, or what they look like?"

Jake closed his eyes tight and held his breath, waiting for Emma to give the deputy details of their earlier encounter.

"I wish I did, but, I've never seen anyone. I can just feel them, and so can Otis."

The tension in Jake's body eased, and he slowly opened his eyes. She wasn't going to give him away after all.

"Otis was really upset a couple nights ago." Emma continued. "He was growling at something in the woods, and I don't think it was just another animal. I think he was scared, and so was I. Then today, he reacted that same way at the festival, and I could swear someone was staring at me, I just couldn't see them."

Emma knew she wasn't telling Matt the whole story, but, she just couldn't right now. Her intuition was telling her not to reveal anything about the mystery man just yet. There was, however, the other presence to contend with, and maybe Matt could help.

"I don't know, Matt, maybe it is just my imagination. I just don't know how to explain Otis' reaction though."

"Well, I think dogs have a pretty good perception of things around 'em, so I'm sure somethin' was out there. The question is what." He took her hands giving them a comforting squeeze. "Tell ya what. I'll check around town to see if anyone has noticed anything out of the ordinary. With the festival going on, there have been a lot of strangers around, and maybe someone noticed somebody that didn't quite belong. In the meantime, keep your doors locked, and try not to worry. I'll let ya know what I find out."

The genuine concern in the deputy's face was obvious and Emma realized just how kind and thoughtful he was. Matt leaned over, giving her a gentle good night kiss. She closed her eyes, hoping to bring the romantic thoughts she had racing through her mind to life. Instead, out of the darkness came two silver stars. As they approached, the mist around them took on the shape of one of the most handsome faces she had ever seen. His face. Quickly opening her eyes, Emma found Matt's face within inches of her own. She looked away, hoping he wouldn't see how guilty she felt.

"Do you want me to check out the house before I leave," he asked her.

"Uh, no, I'm sure everything's okay." Emma's voice sounded shaky to her ears. "I locked it up tight before we left."

"All right. If you're sure?"

"I'm sure."

"Well, I best be goin' then. I think I'll wait though, until you're safe inside."

"I'd appreciate that."

Matt gave her another quick kiss, and then headed for his truck.

"Matt?" He stopped midway down the steps. "Thanks again. I really did have a wonderful time. And, well, thanks for listening to me."

He smiled at her, touching the brim of his hat. "You're more than welcome, ma'am."

Returning his smile, she turned and unlocked the door.

Otis, tiger in mouth, squeezed in ahead of her and headed straight for the couch. Emma gave Matt one last wave, then closed the door securing both locks. She heard the truck start up and head down the lane.

"Out rather late, aren't we?" The deep voice came out of the darkness behind her, causing her to almost knock over the lamp she was attempting to turn on. Her fingers fumbled for the light switch and, finding it, she turned the knob. The old Victorian lamp flooded the living room with a soft, yellow light. Whipping around, she found Jake stretched out on her couch, shirt partly opened, with Otis sitting at his feet.

"What the hell are you doing in my house!" Emma yelled at him.

"Waiting for you to get home. Took you long enough, the party was over hours ago. Where have you been?"

"That's none of your business."

Jake swung himself up into a sitting position and leaned back into the couch. Otis flopped down, nuzzling his head up against the side of Jake's leg.

"Your deputy friend been showing you some of the late night hot spots around town?" Emma could hear the sarcastic edge to his voice.

"What I've been doing is also none of your business."

"I told you I needed to talk to you tonight."

"And, I thought I made it clear that I would talk to you in the morning. Now get the hell out of here."

"No."

"What do you mean no? This is my house, and I want you out." Emma was getting madder by the minute, not only with the good-looking stranger who had apparently made himself at home, but, with her supposed guardian and protector who seemed to have defected to the other side. "You," she said, looking at the dog, "Get off that couch and get your butt over here."

Ignoring her, Otis continued nosing his way up the side of Jake's leg until his head was resting in Jake's lap. Never taking his eyes off Emma, Jake's automatic reflex was to start scratching the dog's chest.

"I don't think he's listening to you. Seems pretty comfortable right where he is."

"You may have won him over, but, you haven't me. And, breaking into my house isn't helping you any. Now, you can either leave, or I'll call the Sheriff's Office. I'm sure they can have Deputy Green back here within just a few minutes."

At the mention of the deputy's name, a dark cloud crossed over Jake's face. Slowly he rose off the couch, taking a deliberate step towards her. "I wouldn't do that if I were you."

Not heeding his subtle warning, Emma said, "Well, you're not me, and this isn't your house, it's mine. I'm going to give you one last chance to leave before I pick up that phone."

"Not until you hear what I have to say."

"That's it! I warned you, Mr. McLean."

Emma turned, stomping off towards the kitchen. Reaching around the side of the door, she snatched the handset from the wall phone, and started dialing the number to the Sheriff's Office. She had only punched in two numbers when she felt his body encompass her. He stretched around her, pushing down on the switch and disconnecting the phone. She tried to turn to face him, but, Jake had her pinned between his body and the wall. His hand slid down the length of her arm with a calculated slowness, closing over her hand that still contained the phone. Without removing it from Emma's grasp, he maneuvered both of their hands up the wall, forcing her to hang it up. Jake stepped back just enough to turn her toward him. Letting go of her hand, he placed both of his on the wall, one on each side of her. As he once again moved in towards her, she tried to back away, only to find there was nowhere to go. Looking ahead, Emma found herself staring at his massive chest. Common sense told her she should be frightened, yet, all she could think of at that particular moment was how muscular and smooth his chest was, and how much she wanted to touch him.

"I told you not to do that." His voice was low and quiet, and she could feel his breath move the curls on the top of her head. Trying to compose herself, she swallowed hard and looked up.

"You're a stranger who has broken into my home. What did you expect me to do?"

"I expected you to trust me."

"Trust you!" Emma looked at him in astonishment. "You try to kidnap me at the dance, then you scare me to death in my own home, and you expect me to trust you?"

"Yes, I do."

Looking down, Emma voice became such a soft whisper that he almost missed her words. "How do I know you're not the one who's here to hurt me?"

Placing his finger under her chin, Jake tilted her head up. She was scared. He could see it in her face. And, yet, the look she gave him said she wanted to believe him, wanted to trust him. With a gentle touch, he brushed her cheek with the back of his fingers.

"Trust me, I could never hurt you."

Cupping her chin in his hand, Jake lowered his head, brushing his lips against hers. Emma's mouth reacted with a slight movement in response to his. Increasing the pressure of his kiss, he felt her tense, as if she might bolt any minute. Not wanting to spook her, but needing to possess her, he moved his hand from her chin, around to the back of her neck, entangling his fingers in her hair. Jake continued to prolong the kiss, his demanding tongue probing her lips, looking for an opening. His other arm had slipped around her waist, and he was making small, sensuous circles on the small of her back. Her tension eased, and she melted against him. Emma's hands were moving their way up his torso, stopping a moment at his chest before encircling his neck. The assault on her lips from his insistent tongue was taking its toll, and she started to part her lips. Jake wasted no time in accepting the invitation, no matter how small it might be. What little reasoning he had left told him to take it slow, however, he couldn't stop himself. His skillful tongue slipped past her trembling lips, claiming what was his.

The air surrounding them crackled with the hot electrical current she had been experiencing all day. Emma could feel the heat from Jake's body penetrate the silky material of her dress. Her lips were on fire as his tongue explored in depth the warmth of her mouth. Maneuvering her hands down the front of his open shirt, Emma started to examine the hard, sculptured muscles of his chest and shoulders, detecting their underlying power. A muffled groan escaped from Jake's throat as her fingers brushed across his firm, flat stomach before encircling his waist. His hand that had been stroking her back now moved up, tracing the contours of her side. As he cupped her breast, she felt her nipple harden under his thumb, straining against the confining material of her dress. Trapping her tighter between his body and the wall, Emma could feel every point where their bodies touched. Her breasts were buried against Jake's chest, and he had pinned her thighs against the wall with his own. She became aware of the hardness of him against her stomach, and she knew he wanted her. Placing his hands on her shoulders, Jake pushed the straps of her dress down the sides of her arms. His feather light touch on her bare skin made her tingle, and Emma could feel herself losing control. She was starting to drift away, when a small, subtle voice reached out, reminding her of the possible danger she might be in, and her eyes flew open.

Jake sensed the immediate change in her body. Her hands withdrew from under his shirt and, though it was almost impossible to do so, she tried to flatten herself even more against the wall, attempting to put some space between them. Releasing her lips from his, he looked down into her eyes that were clouded with uncertainty. Jake knew he had not been mistaken in reading the signals her body had given him. There was no doubt Emma wanted him as much as he wanted her, however, it was also clear that something was frightening her. Not wanting it to be him, he let her go, backing up towards the middle of the living room.

For several minutes Emma remained where she was. Wrapping her arms around herself, and taking a deep breath, she hoped to still the shivers that continued to run through her. The old house was cool, but, the temperature of the room was not what was causing her to shake. She was scared of him, or perhaps better put, she was scared of the feelings he aroused in her, ones she hadn't experienced in a very long time. Martha Quinn had warned her that tonight was going to be one of confusion, and confused she was. Emma studied the gorgeous stranger standing in her living room, trying to decide whether to trust him, and what her next move should be. Regaining her composure, she moved away from the wall. Jake watched her as she skirted around him heading toward the stairs.

Otis, who up to this point had been pretty much ignoring everything, now kept an eye on his mistress. Lowering his front feet off the couch, he gave a leisurely stretch and then padded over to where Jake was standing. Nosing his hand, Otis insisted on being petted good night. Obliging the dog, Jake scratched him behind the ear, all the while keeping his eyes on Emma. Nuzzling Jake one more time, the dog walked over to Emma and leaned up against her leg.

"Emma." It was the first time Jake had used her name since she met him. His voice was deep and husky, and she liked the way her name sounded when he spoke. "We still need to talk. It's really important that you know what's going on."

The look on his face told her that he was worried, but, she knew that she could no longer be near him tonight. She was certain that if the evening were to continue they might wind up doing much more than talking by the time daylight came.

"Mr. McLean, it's been a very long day for me. I promise that you will have my undivided attention in the morning, but, for now, I'm going to bed."

Jake remained silent. He made no attempt to go near her, and he also made no attempt to leave.

Resigning herself to the fact that Jake was going to do whatever he wanted to, yet, still trying to retain some shred of control of her own, Emma said, "I trust that since you found your own way into my house, that you will be able to find your own way out. Good night, Mr. McLean."

With Otis at her side, Emma turned and climbed the stairs to her bedroom. While closing the bedroom door, she saw the light from the living room disappear as the lamp was turned off. Climbing into bed, she scooted down under the lilac comforter. She could feel Otis stretched out across the foot of her bed, and she wiggled her cold toes under his body, absorbing his warmth. Images of the day's events replayed themselves over and over in her mind, always ending up at the same place, with her in Jake's arms. Just as sleep finally overtook her, Emma realized that she never did hear him leave.

# Chapter Fifteen

She was floating down a long hallway decorated with expensive works of art. A massive door at the end of the hall beckoned to her. Emma's heart was pounding so hard she thought it might explode, and the sound of it reverberated in her ears. She wanted to turn back, to run away forever from this place, however, for some unexplainable reason she just couldn't. Everything around her was out of focus except for the door. Watching from outside herself, Emma turned the gold plated handle and floated into the room. The scene was always the same. Clothes were scattered around the floor, a fire was burning low in the fireplace, and a crystal bedside lamp was on. In the background, a faint pulsing sound could be heard, due to the phone being off the hook. The body on the bed was laying on top of crimson colored sheets. Wanting to resist, yet, unable to do so, she moved toward the bed. Emma tried to will herself awake, but, as many times before, her hand reached out and rolled the body over. Usually upon discovering it was Charles, and seeing the enormous number of stab wounds to his body, she would scream and wake up. Tonight that automatic response was stifled as the dream took a different turn. Lifting her head up from the gruesome scene before her, Emma glimpsed at what appeared to be a face reflected in the old fashioned mirror above the bed. Sensing something dark and sinister behind her, she caught the movement of a shadow passing in front of the fireplace right before it seemed to disappear into the wall. A sweet smell, she knew but couldn't seem to identify, hung in the room. Looking back one more time at Charles' body, it was the first time in her dreams she ever allowed herself to see the vacant sockets where his eyes used to be.

Emma woke up in a cold sweat. The dream hadn't been a part of her life for several months now, and it frightened her that it had returned. This new version was particularly terrifying. Still shivering, Emma got out of bed and headed for the bathroom. She needed a hot shower to help soothe the fears that had invaded both her mind and body. Opening the bedroom door, Emma was hit with the luscious aroma of fresh brewed coffee wafting its way up from the kitchen. Someone was moving about downstairs, and there was no doubt in her mind who it was. She started for the stairs, then changed her mind turning into the bathroom instead. After that dream, she needed a shower before facing him.

\* \* \*

Jake had been awake for a couple of hours. Using the guest bath downstairs, he'd managed to take a shower without disturbing Emma. He had waited as long as possible before breaking down, and making himself a pot of coffee. Sitting at the kitchen table drinking his first cup, he reflected on the events of the previous evening. Jake vowed not to let his emotions, or hormones, run amok today. He had to stay focused on the business at hand, which was first and foremost Emma's safety. Hearing her moving about on the floor above, he had expected to see her come blazing into the kitchen demanding to know why he was here. Instead, the sound of the shower drifted down from the upstairs bath. From behind him came the sound of toenails clicking their way across the hardwood floor. The big lab, shaking off the last bit of sleep, lazily wandered into the kitchen and plopped himself down beside Jake's chair.

"You look like you need coffee as much as I do." Otis' only response was the slow wagging of his tail across the linoleum.

"How do you feel about some breakfast then?" The dog didn't move a muscle, except to speed up the wagging of his tail. "I'll take that as a yes."

Jake got up from the table and started rummaging through the cabinets, finding plates, silverware, and pans. Taking a peek in the refrigerator, he saw that Emma had bacon and eggs. Recalling the morning he woke up hungry in her barn, and how good the smell of frying bacon was, he grabbed the package of meat, along with some eggs, and headed for the stove.

\* \* \*

She stood in the door of the kitchen watching him fix breakfast. He appeared to be no stranger to cooking, munching away at the plate of bacon on the counter as he fixed the eggs. It had been a very long time since a man had spent the night in her house, and even longer since one had fixed her breakfast. Emma knew any logical person would be upset with him, yet, somehow she felt reassured by his presence. The dream had left an uneasiness inside her, and it was comforting to know someone else was around.

"Well, Mr. McLean, I see you've managed to make yourself right at home," Emma said, heading for the coffee pot.

Startled, Jake turned from the stove. He hadn't heard her

come down stairs, and she hadn't gone out of her way to let him know she was there. She was dressed in black shorts and a sunny yellow T-shirt. Her wavy hair was still wet from her shower, and he noticed she was barefoot. Coffee in hand, Emma made her way to the back door, opening it up and letting in the fresh morning air.

"My name's Jake, and just how long have you been standing there?" he asked, reaching for another piece of smoke meat.

"Long enough to wonder if you had any intention of sharing that bacon."

"You're lucky that I haven't finished eating, done the dishes, and put everything away by now. I thought you were never gonna get up."

"I had a long day yesterday, and I needed my beauty sleep." Sipping her coffee, Emma gave him a small smile, then took a seat at the table. "You must have gotten up awfully early this morning in order to break into my house again."

"Who said I broke in again?" Jake glanced over his shoulder at her. Emma's guess that he had never left last night had been right. Dishing the eggs onto two plates, he divided up the remaining bacon. Adding some toast to the plates, Jake set one down in front of Emma and then took a seat across from her.

"Well, I trust that you were comfortable at least."

"You have a very nice guest room and bath, and you'll be happy to know that I cleaned up after myself."

"I suppose that's the least you could do, considering you weren't exactly invited."

Letting her comment slide, Jake got up and retrieved the coffee pot from the counter.

"Would you like some more before I polish off this pot?"

"Yeah, thanks."

They ate breakfast in relative quiet, interjecting small talk once in a while when the silence got too awkward. When Jake had first seen Emma this morning, he had noticed right away how pale and troubled she seemed to be. He'd questioned himself if it was due to his being there, but, it hadn't taken him long to realize it was something else. Jake could only hope he would be able to gain Emma's trust enough for her to confide in him. Observing her from across the table, she seemed to be relaxing somewhat and the color was starting to return to her face. After they finished eating, Emma started to clean up, when a small bark escaped from Otis, who was eyeing the dishes in her hand.

"You didn't think I'd forget you, did you?" Emma said, smiling down at the big dog. His tail whipped back and forth, and Emma tossed him the last piece of bacon on her plate. Appearing to be satisfied, Otis laid back down under the table.

"Want some help with the dishes?" Jake offered.

"Oh, you do dishes, too?"

"When you're a bachelor you only have one of everything, so if you don't do dishes, you don't eat." Without knowing it, Jake had just answered another question that had been plaguing Emma's mind—he was single.

Between the both of them, they had the kitchen cleaned up in no time, and Jake put on another pot of coffee. Once it had finished brewing, he poured them each a cup and they settled in once more at the big, oak table. The time had come for the conversation that neither of them was looking forward to having.

"Emma, first off, I want you to know that I didn't mean to frighten you yesterday. I was concerned for your safety and wanted to keep an eye on you all the time. I know my approach to you was a little unorthodox, but, I really needed to talk with you."

"A little unorthodox? That's rather an understatement, isn't it?

Or, do you always break into people's homes when you have a sudden urge to talk?"

"Maybe I should've waited until this morning to contact you, but, I couldn't, not after yesterday."

"What about yesterday?"

"I wasn't the only one watching you, but, then you knew that didn't you?"

Emma stared out the back door, giving him a small nod. She recalled the cold wind that had surrounded her at the dance. Directing her attention back to Jake, she asked, "So, how do I know I can trust you? How do I know you're not lying to me?"

"As far as trusting me, that's something you'll just have to figure out for yourself. As far as lying to you, all I can tell you is that I'm not, and I'll answer any questions you have."

"Okay. Who hired you to watch me?"

"Can't answer that."

A look of exasperation, mixed with annoyance, crossed Emma's face. "You just said you would answer any question I had."

"I would if I could, but I can't."

"Don't give me any of this client confidentiality crap. I want to know who hired you."

"Emma, I can't tell you because I don't know."

"You don't know?" Emma said, expressing the disbelief that was covering her face. "Are you in the habit of working for people you don't even know?"

"Not generally, but, your case was different."

"Different? Different how?"

"When this anonymous client first e-mailed me, I wasn't too sure I wanted the case. I just knew when I told them what my fee would be, that they'd go somewhere else, but, they didn't. And, what can I say, I needed the money. At the same time, they seemed to have a genuine concern for your safety, so I did a little digging into your background."

"Did you find anything interesting?"

"Your name rang a bell. Then I remembered who your husband was, and that he had been murdered."

At the mention of her husband's death, Jake noticed Emma turning pale, as the dream from the previous night took shape in her mind.

"Emma, are you all right?" His voice was soft.

Clearing her throat a little, she answered, "Yes, I'm fine, go on."

"Well, I studied your husband's file. A lot of things don't add up to him surprising a burglar, and the police are remaining pretty tight lipped about why the investigation was dropped. Then, while I was looking at your picture, I got this funny feeling in my gut that perhaps my client was right, that you were in danger. So, I took the case without ever finding out who was paying the bill."

"How long have you been watching me?"

"About three months or so."

"And, how long has Oats known you were around?" Emma asked, affectionately stroking the dog's back with her bare foot.

"A couple of months. He keeps a secret pretty well, don't you think?" Jake gave her a crooked smile that made her heart jump.

Returning his smile, she said, "Yeah, he does. You know, I think he wanted us to meet long before now."

"Emma, do have any idea who might have killed your husband?" Jake's tone was serious again.

"Not really, but, I've always thought it was someone who knew him, and that it was personal."

"What makes you say that?"

"The house wasn't broken into. The police said there was no sign of forced entry. Also, he'd taken off his clothes, like he was getting ready for bed. The police tried to say that the burglar was in another part of the house and snuck up on him, but, I just don't believe that. Nothing was missing from the house, except—" Emma's voice trailed off.

"Except for what, Emma?"

"Charles' wedding band. It was the only thing missing. They never did find it."

"I must have missed that in the police report somewhere."

"I don't think they put it in the report. It wasn't until the funeral director asked me if I wanted Charles to be buried with it, that I knew it was gone. When I asked the police about it, they said the ring probably came off in transit to the morgue, and they didn't pursue it any further."

"You said you thought the motive was personal. Why?"

Again, Emma caught herself thinking about the dream. Goose bumps covered her arms and legs. "I guess because of the condition of the body. Why would a burglar go to those lengths to mutilate it? That never made sense to me."

"Or me. So, why do you think the police shut down the investigation?"

"Aaron Bellecek."

"Aaron Bellecek. He was a partner of your husband's, right?"

"Yes. He's the senior partner at Charles' law firm. He's quite powerful, and has lots of contacts down at City Hall. I don't think he wanted that kind of publicity for the firm, and since they weren't having much luck finding any evidence or suspects, I'm pretty sure Aaron just had the investigation halted. He probably figured the firm could gain some sympathy if the story was that Charles was just in the wrong place at the wrong time. Aaron didn't want people thinking that any of the firm's clientele could possibly have that kind of vendetta against them."

"Do you think it was a client of Charles'?"

"Maybe. I've thought about that a lot. Charles wasn't one of the most popular people around, and he was vicious in the courtroom. Compassion wasn't one of his better qualities. I suppose it also could've been someone who lost a case because of him." Emma paused before continuing. "But, somewhere deep down, I still believe it was even something more personal than that."

Jake could tell by Emma's expression that there was more she wanted him to know. Not wanting to push her, but, needing more answers to the puzzle, Jake asked her, "Emma, was Charles having an affair?"

She looked at him, somewhat embarrassed. "I think so, but, I don't know for sure. I tried to convince myself he wasn't, but, most of the signs were there."

"Do you have any idea who it was?"

"I'm not even sure there was only one. Women were always coming onto him, and I'm sure his ego wouldn't have let him turn them down."

Jake hesitated a moment. "What about you?" he asked, obviously uncomfortable with the question.

"What about me?"

"Were you having an affair?" He hated asking her that, yet, he needed to know.

The question took her by surprise. Her marriage vows had been important to her, and she had never even so much as entertained the idea of cheating on Charles. When things had gotten bad between them, she still stood beside him, trying to be supportive, to be a good wife. No one else had entered her mind, no one...except maybe David. She and David had had a connection, however, Emma had never allowed it go any farther than just good friends, and neither had he. From the perceptive look Jake was giving her, she knew the expression on her face must be giving away her thoughts.

"No, I never had an affair." The underlying anger in her voice was so strong Jake knew he had hit a nerve.

"Are you telling me the truth, Emma?"

"Yes, I'm telling you the truth," she said heatedly. "I never cheated on my husband, and I'm insulted that you asked!"

Emma started to rise from her chair. Jake's hand shot out and grabbed her arm, stopping her. His cool, grey eyes held her's for several moments, studying her. "If you never had an affair, why are you so angry with me for asking the question?"

"Aren't we supposed to trust and believe each other," she spat sarcastically.

"I do believe you, but, there's more to it than you're telling me."

With a sigh of defeat, Emma sat back down. She could never imagine that David would ever hurt anyone, least of all her. However, her mind drifted back to the night of Charles' murder, and the fight between him and David. Emma had never seen David so angry before. She had to admit that once or twice she'd wondered if David might have been involved in some way with Charles' death. She'd never told the police about the argument, wanting to believe, in her mind, that David had not been capable of such a thing. Could she have been wrong? With Jake staring at her so intently, she now knew she needed to tell him everything.

"His name is David Meyers. We never had an affair, but, he worked for Charles and we developed a close friendship."

A tiny spark of jealousy flared up in Jake's stomach, and he had to remind himself to concentrate on the task at hand. "Emma, I don't want to pry, but, it would be a big help if you could tell me about him, and what kind of relationship you two had."

Taking a deep breath, Emma told Jake everything she could remember. How they met, how their friendship developed, David's crush on her, and his determination to protect her from

Charles, even to the point of putting his job on the line. She told Jake about the fight that took place the evening Charles died, and why she hadn't told the police. As Jake listened to Emma's story, he could feel a connection with David. Through personal experience, he knew how easy it was to become addicted to her and, once so, the desire to possess and protect her could be overpowering. But, could that desire be so powerful as to make someone commit murder? Jake knew the answer was yes. He had seen that scenario a number of times in his law enforcement days.

"Do you still feel that he couldn't have murdered Charles?"

"I don't know anymore. I hoped by moving here that I wouldn't have to think about it ever again. But, now, I've not only got you watching me, but, maybe some psycho, and those damn dreams have started again, too."

Her comment piqued his curiosity. "What dreams?"

"They're nightmares really. About the night I found Charles." The same pained expression from earlier in the morning was again on her face.

"You wanna tell me about 'em?"

Emma hated having to recall the dream, yet, maybe by telling him about it would alleviate the uneasiness she felt. She told Jake the whole story of that evening, from the time she got home, to actually finding Charles' body in the bedroom. Then she told him of her dreams and how, up until last night, they had always been the same. Emma explained to him that the image of a face in the mirror and the sweet fragrance were new additions to the nightmare. It was as if her subconscious was trying to tell her that she knew more than she thought she did. But why now. If she had known something all along, why was it just now surfacing. Emma knew the answer, and it was sitting right across the table from her. Jake had been here last night, protecting her. Somewhere in the depth of her mind, she had finally felt safe, safe enough to let what was buried start to dig its way out. In her heart, she knew that he would never let anything happen to her.

"Jake?" Her voice was unsteady. "Do you think I know who it was that killed Charles, and I just can't remember?"

"I don't know, Em. But, if that secret is hiding somewhere in that pretty, little head of yours, we need to unlock it."

"What I don't understand is, if they were there and they wanted me dead, why didn't they kill me that night? Why now?"

"There could be a lot of reasons. Maybe they never really wanted you dead. Maybe they didn't think you saw them that night, but, started worrying later that you did. Who knows? But they'll have to come through me first before they can get to you." The hard set look in Jake's eyes told Emma he meant every word of what he said.

"Well, I certainly hope it doesn't come to that because I'm kind of getting used to you being around."

# Chapter Sixteen

Danny Taylor heard his mother's voice, as he ran out the back door, threatening to tan his hide if he got his good church clothes dirty before they were ready to leave. Like most eleven-year old boys, he wasn't looking forward to spending this beautiful, sunny morning listening to some long, drawn-out sermon. Knowing that's what he'd be doing for the next couple of hours, he wanted to check on what he'd found in the old barn yesterday afternoon, and make sure it was still there. Halloween was coming up soon, and he and his older brother, Mark, were going to throw the best holiday party in town. Mark had been teasing Danny for several days now that he was planning something very spooky and creepy, but, refused to tell what it was. Yesterday, however, Danny had found what Mark was hiding.

At one time, the Taylor's home had been a working farm, but, now it sat within the city limits of Cedar Falls. The old barn was a relic of the past and never used anymore, except to store lawn and garden supplies. Danny's late father had thought of replacing it with a modern garage, but, Mrs. Taylor always loved the memories residing in those weathered, grey walls, and had never allowed it to be torn down. The boys had spent many hours playing in the hayloft and building forts in the empty stalls. There was a door at the back of the barn leading to a tack room that hadn't been used in years. That's where Danny had discovered what was going to be Mark's surprise, however, Danny had a surprise of his own. The bright sunlight flowed in behind him as he walked through the big barn door. On his way to the back of the barn, he stopped at the last stall nearest the tack room, dragging out an old scarecrow. Upon entering the tack room, a grin spread across his face from ear to ear. It was still here. Sitting in the middle of the shadowy room was a coffin.

Danny was pretty sure Mark was intending to use the coffin to scare him and his friends at the Halloween party, so Danny was determined to get him first. Kneeling down, he took a bottle of ketchup out of his coat pocket, shook it up, and then squeezed it onto the chest and head of the scarecrow. He was feeling so proud of himself, he didn't even care that his mother was going to be mad because he got some on his good clothes. This was going to be great. For once he'd beat Mark to the punch. Danny picked up the scarecrow and propped it up against the end of the coffin. Opening the lid, he a felt chill that made the little hairs on the back of his neck stand up. He was sure someone was watching him. Turning around, Danny surveyed the tack room, then looked out the door into the barn. Finding no one there, he shrugged and turned back to the coffin, peeking inside. The scarecrow was never going to fit. The coffin just wasn't big enough for two.

# Chapter Seventeen

Matt was enjoying his regular Sunday morning breakfast at the Cedar Falls Café more than usual today. Maggie, as always, was teasing him and giving him a hard time. In her usual attire of jeans and a T-shirt, with her hair once again pulled back into a French roll, she was attractive, yet, Matt couldn't get the sexy image of the way she looked last night out of his head. He'd always known that Maggie was a smart, strong woman, he just never realized how truly beautiful she was. He was seeing her in a whole new light and was liking what he saw. Maybe what he'd been searching for had been here under his nose all along. A picture of that gorgeous, auburn hair flowing over those creamy shoulders filled Matt's mind, and he grinned.

"You gonna let me in on the joke?" Maggie's sultry voice brought him back to the present.

"Joke?" Matt stammered, "Uh, what joke?"

"Well, I figured somethin' must be funny by the way you were grinnin' to yourself over here."

"Just day dreamin' I guess."

"Well, I hope they were sweet ones." Maggie winked at him, leaving to make the rest of her rounds.

"You can be sure they were," Matt muttered under his breath.

Matt observed Maggie while she talked and laughed with the other customers, making her way from table to table. The sway of her hips reminded him of how well they had seemed to fit together dancing last night. At that moment, he knew he would be spending more time with her, maybe the rest of his life. His eyes followed her as she came back around the counter heading his way.

"Need a refill?" Maggie asked, filling up his cup before he could answer.

"Yeah, thanks. Uh, Maggie?"

"Hmm?"

"I was wonderin'—"

"Wonderin' what?"

Pausing, Matt's glance was drawn to a lovely pair of lavender eyes. "I was just thinkin', maybe…" the squawk of his police radio interrupted him. Pulling the radio off his belt, Matt depressed the key and answered.

"This is Matt."

"Sorry to ruin your breakfast, Matt, but, Mike wants you to check somethin' out over at the Taylor place."

"What's going on, Sherry?"

Sherry had been the dispatcher at the Sheriff's Office for nearly twenty years. Being almost forty-five years old, didn't change the fact that her high pitched, squeaky voice made her sound like she was still a teenager.

"Don't know for sure, Mrs. Taylor said somethin' about a coffin being in her barn."

Chuckling a little, Matt said, "Okay. I'm leavin' right now. Over and out."

"A coffin?" Maggie asked. "What in the world is a coffin doin' in the Taylor's barn?"

"It's probably just some kids pullin' a Halloween prank. An old coffin was stolen from Anderson's mortuary the other night. We figured it would show up sooner or later."

"You want me to wrap up the rest of your breakfast to take with you?"

"No, thanks. But, I would appreciate some coffee to go."

"Comin' right up."

Maggie filled up two Styrofoam cups with coffee. "Just in case you're out there a while."

"Well, thanks. How much are the damages?"

"It's on the house today."

"On the house? What did I do to deserve that?"

"*You* didn't do anything. I'm just in a very good mood today, so you'd better take advantage of it."

"Well, the least I can do is leave you a tip."

"Why don't you just take me out sometime, and we'll call it even."

Maggie stifled back a laugh when she saw the shocked expression on Matt's face. A pink blush was creeping its way into his cheeks, and it was obvious he was at a loss for words.

"That *is* what you were gonna ask me a couple of minutes ago, isn't it? To go out, I mean." Maggie gave him a flirtatious smile.

"Uh, yeah, it was."

"Then I accept."

Matt's charming, boyish face blossomed into a smile. Balancing one of the cups of coffee on top of the other, he started for the door. "I'll give you a call a little later on."

"I'll be here."

Maggie watched Matt through the café window until he disappeared into his patrol car. Humming to herself, she was clearing the dishes off the counter, when out of the corner of her eye she saw one of the customers get up from the booth, leave some money on the table, and follow Matt out the door. Generally, that wouldn't have seemed unusual, but, this same customer had come in right behind Matt this morning, and was a stranger in town. While taking their order, Maggie had gotten the creepy feeling that the person she was talking to was looking right through her, focusing on the deputy. A shiver ran up Maggie's back as she remembered the cold, dead look in the customer's eyes. Her train of thought was broken as one of her other customers caught her attention, and waved her over.

While making her rounds, coffee pot in hand, Maggie's thoughts returned to Matt. Last night she'd had felt a definite spark between herself and Matt, and so had he. She cherished her friendship with Emma, however, her woman's intuition told her that Emma's interest in Matt was purely platonic. Maggie felt that Emma's romantic interests lay elsewhere. She remembered Emma's reaction when the tall, dark stranger had appeared outside the cafe, and she and Sara had seen the same man at the festival yesterday. Emma didn't appear to know him, yet Maggie was sure he was playing some kind of part in Emma's life. She'd have to talk to her about it next time she saw her, but in the meantime, Maggie had her own needs to consider. This morning, she decided that instead of continuing to wait in the wings to see what Matt was going to do, she would just give him a little nudge, and see which way he'd fall. She had taken a chance, and it had paid off.

* * *

Matt pulled up in the circular drive in front of the Taylor's home. Danny, Mark, and Amanda Taylor were sitting on the porch, eyes intently focused on the barn. Matt never noticed the other pair of eyes that had followed him out of the cafe, and were now parked down the street in a plain, white car. Waving at the three of them, the deputy walked over to the house.

"So, Mrs. Taylor, I hear you have a coffin in your barn." Figuring this to be nothing more than a Halloween prank, Matt was trying to keep the atmosphere light, until he noticed how ghost white Amanda's face was. Still shaking, she was holding tightly onto the two boys.

"Amanda, what's wrong?" Concern flooded Matt's voice as he realized the situation had taken a serious turn.

Taking her eyes away from the barn, she looked at Matt, horror written all over her face. "There's something in there."

"In the barn?"

"No, in the coffin. Danny found it this morning."

"What is it?"

"I don't know. A body, I think."

"Why don't show me where it's at?"

"No, I'm not going back in there, and neither are the boys." Amanda's voice made it clear there was no room for negotiation.

"Okay, okay. Ya'll stay here, and I'll take a look. Where abouts in the barn is it?"

"Clear in the back. There's a tack room back there, and that's where it's at."

"All right, I'll check it out and be back in a minute."

Matt turned and walked across the yard to the barn. Stepping through the door from the warm sunshine into the cool shadows, he again was unaware of the eyes that were now watching him from a dark corner of the barn. Matt drew his gun, moving towards the back of the barn, checking each stall along the way. Arriving at the door to the tack room, he stepped across the threshold and found a coffin sitting on some hay bales in the middle of the room. The lid was off, lying on the ground, and beside it was the scarecrow that Danny had dropped. Matt made a number of mental notes while examining the interior of the room. There were no puddles, or traces, of blood that he could see anywhere, and nothing seemed out of the norm except, of course, for the coffin itself. Light in the tack room was dim, so Matt pulled a small flashlight from his belt. Shining the beam into the coffin, it didn't take long for the blood to drain from his face when he saw what the coffin contained. In all his years on the force, he'd never seen anything like this. His stomach churned, and he knew that he wasn't going to be able to keep his breakfast down. Stumbling out the door, Matt buckled to his knees in one of the horse stalls, emptying his stomach of its contents. The eyes watched him, knowing full well what the deputy had found in the coffin, for they had put it there. They'd known that sooner or later this discovery was going to be made, but, hoped it wouldn't have been for another day, or so.

Regaining some strength in his legs, Matt sat back on his heels, resting until a wave of dizziness passed. Leaving the barn, he headed straight for his patrol car. Picking up the radio, he called into the office reaching the squeaky-voiced dispatcher.

"Sherry, this is Matt. I need to talk to Mike right now." Both his voice and hands were shaking.

"You okay, Matt?" she asked.

"Just get Mike, *now!*" Matt worked on calming his nerves. It felt like hours before someone came back on the radio.

"What's goin' on over there, Matt?" It was the gruff voice of Sheriff Mike Henderson.

"You need to get over here with a crime scene kit. And, I need you to call the coroner's office, and tell 'em to get over here, too."

"I take it you've found somethin'."

"Yeah, I found somethin'. There's a body in the coffin."

"What?!"

"I said, there's a body in the coffin."

"Male or female?"

"I don't know."

"What do ya mean ya don't know?"

Turning another shade whiter, Matt said, "The body's such a mess, I can't tell what it is."

There was a long, deafening pause before Mike's voice came back on. "Stay put, I'm on my way."

Mike didn't have to worry about Matt staying put. He had no intention of going back into that barn without his boss at his side.

The eyes watched the deputy talking on his radio as they headed back to the white car down the street. They had overheard enough of the deputy's conversation with the waitress this morning to realize that the deputy's romantic interest might be veering away from Emma. That realization should've given them some relief, but it didn't. They had been jealous of the attention the deputy had shown Emma, and, now, as strange as it might be, they felt irritation at the fact he seemed to have no regard for her feelings, and could so quickly pursue another woman. Emma was a good person, and deserved to have someone who could be faithful to her. It was evident that either way, the deputy was not to escape the wrath developing in the cold, depth of those eyes.

# Chapter Eighteen

Jake and Emma talked well into the afternoon. She told Jake everything starting from when she joined the firm, up until she left and moved to Missouri. Jake questioned her about everyone who had worked for the firm, and what their relationship to Charles might have been. There had been a couple of employees who Charles had fired in the past few years, but, she'd convinced Jake that she really didn't think any of them were angry enough to kill him. After finishing with the employee list, he started asking her about the cases Charles had been working on, and what his various clients were like. By mid-afternoon they were only about one-quarter of the way through the list that Emma had come up with. They still had quite a ways to go, but, she was starting to feel drained.

"Jake, I need to stop talking about this for a while. How about we take a break, okay?" Her voice sounded tired, and there was a mixture of defeat and sadness in her eyes when she looked at him. As much as he wanted to accommodate her, he had a terrible feeling in his gut that whatever game they were involved in was quickly coming to an end.

"Em, I know you're tired, however, the sooner we get through these cases the sooner we may have some idea of who we're dealing with."

"I know, but, I really need a break. Can we pick this back up after we have some dinner?"

Jake's lips turned up in a mischievous smile. "Are you inviting me to dinner?"

"Thought I might as well, since I figured you'd be here anyway. This way you can leave your lock picking tools at home. By the way, where are you staying?"

"In a little cabin I rented not too far from here."

"I'd like to see it sometime."

Emma didn't fail to notice the peculiar look passing over Jake's face as he thought about all the surveillance equipment that was sitting in the cabin. "You wouldn't be very impressed."

"So, you're trying to impress me now."

"Yeah," he grinned. "How am I doing?"

Sitting back in her chair, arms crossed, Emma gave him the once over. She had to admit to herself he was the most devastatingly, handsome man she'd ever seen. Even with a day's growth of beard and rumpled clothes, that fact was hard to hide. He had impressed her from the first time she saw him watching the house in the early morning shadows. And, although she didn't condone breaking and entering, she was still rather impressed with his determination to see her and talk with her.

"Not too bad, but, you could still work on a few things."

"Okay. I'll just take that as you're not quite ready to get rid of me yet."

Not wanting him to know how close to the truth he was, Emma changed the subject. "So, what do you want for dinner?"

"Anything you fix will be just fine."

"How about steaks then?"

"Steaks sound great." It had been a while since he'd had more than just bologna or peanut butter sandwiches for dinner. A good meal with a beautiful woman, what more could he ask for. "I think I'll go home and clean up a bit. Can I bring anything back with me?"

"Nope, nothin' but the steak." Emma choked back a laugh when she saw the surprised and hesitant expression on his face.

"The steak?" he asked. "Well, uh, sure, okay."

Raising her eyebrows, and giving him a little smile, Emma said, "Only kidding. I just wanted to see what you'd say."

"Well, now you know. I'd go to the ends of the earth to find steak, if it meant being able to have dinner with you."

The tone of Jake's voice was light and teasing, yet, Emma could tell by the steady look in his eyes that he meant what he said. Feeling a little embarrassed, Emma stood up from the table and got a Diet Coke from the refrigerator.

"You want one for the road?" she asked, not turning around as she didn't want to face him yet.

"Sure, I'll take one. Thanks."

Grabbing another can, she closed the door and turned around only to find him standing within inches of her. Swallowing hard, she offered him the soda. He reached out, but, instead of taking the can he pushed a stray, little curl off the side of her face. The back of his fingers caressed her cheek.

"Are you going to be okay here by yourself for the rest of the afternoon?" Both his touch, and the look he gave her belied his concern.

"Don't worry, I'll be fine." She gave him a weak smile.

"I don't like leaving you alone."

"I'm not alone. My guardian angel's laying under the table over there." They both looked over at Otis who hadn't seemed to move a single muscle all day.

Giving her another one of his crooked, little smiles, Jake said, "Kind of a lazy one, isn't he?"

"Most of the time, but, he does have his moments." Their laughter produced only one small wag out of Otis' tail.

Handing him his soda, she walked him to the back door. He leaned over and gave her a quick kiss on her cheek.

"Be back in a few hours, okay?"

"Like I said, I'll be just fine."

Watching him through the screen door, she was rather puzzled when he headed across the yard toward the barn.

"Where are you going?" Her voice brought his attention back around to the house.

"My truck's parked in your barn. I've watched you long enough to know that you never park in there. Figured it was a safe hiding place for last night."

"Oh? And what else do you know about me?"

Probably more than he should, Jake thought to himself. "Only that you're really fond of bacon. See you in a bit."

Jake disappeared into the barn. A few moments later Emma watched as his dark blue Dodge truck pulled out. Waving at her, he headed down the gravel lane. She had to wonder just how much he, in fact, did know about her. Even though they'd only met in person yesterday, he'd been watching her long enough that he'd managed to ingrain himself into her life. Otis' soft fur rubbed up against her leg as the dog leaned into her. Emma knelt down beside him, searching those strange blue eyes for some kind of reassurance.

"Well, Mr. Angel, I sure hope Martha Quinn was right, because I'm putting all my faith in you."

The dog stared back at her, giving her a gentle lick on her cheek, letting her know all was well.

\* \* \*

Deciding to pick up a bottle of wine for dinner, Jake turned towards town when he hit the main road. He was looking forward to spending more time with Emma, he only wished it could be under different circumstances. Maybe after all this was behind them, they could start over again like normal people. Jake pulled into one of the parking spot along the town square. Getting out of the truck, he headed in the direction of Cedar Falls' only liquor store, which was next to the café. Halfway across the street, some sixth sense told him he was being watch. Glancing over his shoulder at his truck, he saw an old woman standing beside it. Still looking behind him, he stepped up onto the sidewalk bumping into someone coming out of the restaurant. Turning around, he found a brilliant pair of lavender eyes checking him out.

"Excuse me. I obviously wasn't watching where I was going." Jake tried not to give any indication that he knew who he was apologizing to.

"That's all right. You seemed a bit preoccupied at the moment." Jake realized that her deep, provocative voice fit her well.

"Yeah, I was watching the old lady across the street."

"What old lady?" asked Maggie, surveying the general direction from which Jake had just come.

"The lady standing right over…there." Jake sounded baffled when he turned around and realized she was gone. "Where'd she go?"

"Sorry, I didn't see anyone, but, then I wasn't really payin' any attention."

Jake knew he wasn't seeing things, she had been there, and she had been watching him. Shaking his head, he apologized once more to Maggie, and started towards the liquor store.

"So, how's Emma?" Maggie's question stopped him in his tracks.

"Pardon me?" Jake swung around to face Maggie, attempting to keep the surprise he felt from showing on his face.

"Emma Hudson. I saw you dancin' with her last night."

How could he have been so stupid as to think no one would have noticed him dancing with Emma? If he'd been thinking straight he would have never gone out onto the dance floor, but, he hadn't been. Being close to her at the time was all that had mattered.

"I'm sorry, you must be mistaken."

"Oh, I'm not mistaken. Trust me, a man like you is hard to miss in this town." The look of confidence on Maggie's face let Jake know that there was no point in trying to bluff her. "Besides, if I'm correct, I don't believe the dance was the first time you noticed Emma. I seem to remember that handsome face of yours watchin' her through my café window."

"You're very observant," replied Jake.

"About you and Emma, or about your handsome face?" Maggie gave him a teasing, sexy smile, and noticed a slight blush creep into his face. "I'm sorry, am I embarrassing you?"

"Perhaps a little," he said, giving her a charming smile that would make any woman melt. No wonder Emma was enchanted by him.

"I had the impression that day at the café that Emma had no idea who you were."

"She didn't."

"So, you actually just met her last night?"

"You could say that."

"How long you been followin' her?"

Jake remained silent. He was starting to get uncomfortable with the direction that this particular conversation was heading.

Maggie looked over at the town square where people were busy taking down their booths and tents from the day before. Returning her gaze to Jake, she looked him straight in the eye.

"You know, Mr.—"

"McLean."

"Mr. McLean. You know this is a pretty quiet town, not much happens around here. The most crime we have is some drunk and disorderlies, and a little petty theft now and then." Maggie paused a moment, giving her words time to sink in. When Jake didn't respond she continued. "Seems this mornin' they found a mutilated body over in the Taylor's barn."

She noticed Jake's face turn pale. "Have they identified the body yet?"

"Not that I know of, but, I'm pretty sure Sheriff Henderson and Deputy Green will be askin' questions around town. With all the people that were here this weekend, they'll be wantin' to know if there's still any strangers around."

For several minutes, Jake's silver gaze and Maggie's lavender one locked in a Mexican standoff. He was trying hard to read her, but, her expression gave nothing away. He made a mental note to himself that he should probably never engage her in a game of poker. Instincts told him that Maggie was probably a tough, but, fair minded woman, and she didn't appear to have judged him yet. Jake had to make a decision now as to how much, if any, he should reveal to her. Finally he spoke.

"I know you don't know me from Adam, and you have no reason to trust me, but, you can't tell the Sheriff about me, not yet."

"Why?" Maggie voice seemed to hold more curiosity than suspicion.

Jake hesitated, hoping he was doing the right thing. "Because I believe Emma's life is in danger, and I can't be there to protect her if I'm spending time in jail answering questions."

"If Emma's in danger, don't you think you *should* tell the Sheriff. After all, that's his job."

"I know that, but, he can't watch her twenty four hours a day. I can."

"Do you think the body they found has anything to do with Emma?"

"Maybe."

Maggie could tell by the look on Jake's face that it was more than maybe. Not knowing exactly why, she decided to go along with him. She'd never been the type to let a handsome face influence her way of thinking, and she knew that wasn't the case now. Still contemplating on why she was making such a decision, it dawned on Maggie it was because of the dog. She'd noticed, both the day at the café and at the dance last night, that Otis had taken quite a shine to this man. She was also aware of the dog's protectiveness of Emma, and if he had accepted this stranger, she would give him a chance, too.

"All right, you have my word I won't say anything. At least for now."

"Thank you. I promise you won't regret it."

"I'd better not, Mr. McLean, or I *will* come looking for you. Emma has become a very close friend of mine, and I would hate to have anything bad happen to her."

"So would I, ma'am, so would I."

Jake could feel anxiety building in his chest, as he looked for the wine. He bought the first bottle of burgundy he came across, and hurried back to his truck. Putting the key in the ignition, he paused before starting the engine as he tried to decide whether to even go back to the cabin and change. If he didn't he was pretty sure Emma would know something was wrong. Looking up, Jake was startled by the face peering at him through the driver's side window. It was the old woman who had been standing by his truck earlier. He also recognized her from the festival yesterday. Her intense black eyes demanded his attention, and he rolled down the window.

"The evil is here, and you must stop it." The voice that resonated from her fragile body was strong and sure.

"Who are you?"

"Most around here would say I'm just a crazy old woman, but, it would do you good to heed my warnin'."

"I saw you at the festival yesterday."

"And, I you. You have been sent here to protect her."

"In a manner of speaking."

"That wasn't a question, my boy. A greater force has made sure you would be here to keep her safe until this evil has been dealt with. You and the dog are her only hope of survival, but, she must first trust you."

"She does trust me." Jake knew he sounded defensive, but couldn't help himself.

"Not completely. She must have no doubts in you if this is to end right."

"Why should she doubt me?"

"You and I both know the answer to that question."

Jake could only stare in silence at the old woman, wondering how much she really knew.

"There is one other thing you should know, my boy."

"What's that?"

"This evil has a face you know. Don't be fooled by it. Don't let it take you by surprise."

With slow, deliberate steps, the old woman walked away from the truck. Disturbed by her prediction, Jake called out to her, "Who's face?"

The old woman continued on her way, never answering, never looking back.

# Chapter Nineteen

Jake returned to Emma's house just as dusk was settling in. He'd gone to the cabin first, shaving, packing a small gym bag with a change of clothes, and checking on the equipment. The tape had shown nothing unusual from the previous night, nor during his absence this afternoon. He'd also checked his computer for messages, finding none. Because the anonymous client had not responded to the latest e-mail he sent, Jake assumed the contract was now canceled, however, he was still uneasy. This particular client had always been prompt in responding to any messages Jake sent, and he had at least expected a confirmation regarding his last communication. He would give them until tomorrow to answer, and if they didn't he would contact them again.

Emma had spent the afternoon puttering around the house, doing some simple household chores, which helped to take her mind off of the current situation. The earlier conversations with Jake had brought back a number of bad memories she'd thought were over and done with. The idea that some dark shadow from her past was stalking her in the present frightened her. Though Emma had barely met him, she suspected Jake was going to be the calm in this upcoming storm. Even during the few hours he was gone, she had missed his presence. Now that he was standing in her kitchen, opening the bottle of wine, she felt better.

"Hope you like what I bought. I don't know much about wine. I'm a beer man myself," Jake said, pouring the deep, ruby colored liquid into two crystal, stemmed glasses.

"You didn't have to get wine for me. A six pack would've been fine."

Turning away from the counter, Jake handed Emma one of the glasses. "Beer didn't seem very romantic."

"Romantic? I thought this was supposed to be a working dinner."

"Well, you just never know how the evening may end."

The lightning hot heat that flashed in his silver eyes made Emma swallow hard. Her body quaked as she remembered how his touch felt from the night before. She'd stopped herself then because she'd been confused and unsure whether to trust him, or not. Somehow she knew that this night could turn out quite different from the last.

Attempting to quell the sexual tension that was beginning to fill the room, she said, "I'm sure you must be getting hungry. I'll put the steaks on."

Jake stepped in front of her, blocking her path to the refrigerator. "I was thinking of just relaxing a bit first. How about sitting out on the porch for a while?"

"Okay."

Walking out onto the front porch, Emma settled into her rocker, and Jake took a seat in the big wicker chair next to her. For a while, neither spoke as they sipped on the wine, and watched the sun descend behind the red and gold laced hills around them.

"This is my favorite time of the day," Emma said dreamily. "It's as if the world is at peace with itself."

"It seems to bring you peace, too."

"And, just how would you know that?"

"I haven't been watching you only in the mornings, you know."

Emma gave him a warm smile. "Didn't you get bored standing out there in the woods all alone?"

"Sometimes. But, then, I wasn't always alone."

"Oh? And, just who was keeping you company?"

"Just someone I met in the woods. I think he's a friend of yours. Black hair, blue eyes, and an annoying habit of always being underfoot."

"Yeah, he's rather demanding, but, he grows on you." Emma gazed with fondness at Otis who was stretched out on the porch, completely blocking the front door.

"Speaking of friends, I bumped into another one of your's today in town."

"Oh, who's that?"

"That sexy looking red head from the café. Don't know her name."

"It's Maggie." There was a touch of jealousy in Emma's voice that Jake had to admit made him feel good. "What did she want?"

"Just asked how you were. Said she saw us together at the dance last night."

"We only danced one dance. I didn't think anyone was paying any attention."

"Your friend indicated that I was pretty hard to miss around town."

Emma had to giggle. "Well, you do kind of stand out. And, just so you know, Maggie's wasn't the only head you turned. Seems, Sara, the young girl at the dart booth, would've given you every prize she had if you'd have just hung around. I believe her exact words were that you were 'quite a hunk'."

Jake couldn't help turning red. He'd always known that women found him attractive, however, he wasn't used to being told so quite this bluntly.

"So, what else did Maggie have to say?" Emma asked.

"Just that I'd better be on my best behavior, or she'd have my hide."

"I wonder what made her ask you about me."

"She said she saw me that day at the café, as well as last night. I think she just wanted to make sure I wasn't some kind of a nut that was out here stalking you."

"Did you tell her about what you were doing here?"

"Enough to keep her from going to the police."

"You know, Jake, maybe we should call the Sheriff. After all, they know everyone around here, and if there was something strange going on they'd be the first to know."

Jake thought about the dead body that Maggie had eluded to earlier. He was uncertain as to whether to tell Emma. She still didn't know him well enough, and he didn't want to take the chance she might suspect him. He would wait.

"I think we need to continue with what we started this morning. If we come up with something substantial, then we'll call them."

"Is there some reason you don't want the Sheriff to know about you?"

"No." Jake hesitated. "Well, maybe. Look, Em, I'm a stranger around here, and I've obviously been following you around. Who do you think they're going to suspect first, someone they can't find, or someone they can get their hands on? I need to be here around the clock to protect you, and I can't do that from a jail cell. You're just going to have to trust me."

Emma knew he was right. She stared up into the sky, continuing to rock back and forth, sipping on her wine. The first star of the evening had appeared. Thinking back to her childhood days, Emma remembered those warm summer nights, lying in the grass, watching those sparkling lights pop up one at a time out of the inky blackness. She had believed, back then, in all of the magic and power that the universe held. Her marriage to Charles had almost changed all of that. He had taken much of the magic out of her world, leaving her to question if such things really existed. With the recent turn of events, she was now allowing herself to believe again. Why had both Jake and Martha Quinn appeared in her life at the same time? Closing her eyes, she let herself wander through a maze of memories. Upon opening them again, she could feel, more than see, Jake watching her as darkness enveloped the porch.

"What are you thinking about?" Jake's voice was as soft as the shadows surrounding them.

"Just wishing upon a star." If Jake could've have seen her, he would have noticed the impish smile playing across her lips.

"What'd you wish for?"

"If I tell you, it won't come true."

"Have anything to do with me?" A touch of amusement tinged his voice.

"I can't tell you that."

"You really must want whatever it is you wished for."

She didn't answer him because she didn't want him to know just how right he was. Changing the subject she said, "Think I'll start dinner."

"Can I help?"

"Sure. You want to cook the steaks, or toss the salad?"

"The steaks of course. Don't you know the man always does the cooking when it involves fire?"

"They teach you that in Neanderthal 101?"

"Yeah." He flashed her a captivating smile. "And, if you're good, maybe I'll show you my cave paintings later."

Laughing, they left the porch and headed for the kitchen. While she made the rest of the dinner, Emma watched Jake through the screen door. He was sitting on the railing of the back deck, another glass of wine in hand, getting up every so often to check on the steaks. Otis had insisted on staying out there with him, even when Emma tried to tempt him back inside with one of his favorite treats. She could see Jake talking to the dog, but, couldn't hear what he was saying. Otis watched intently, as if they were in some deep philosophical discussion. After setting the table, Emma walked over and leaned against the door jam, talking to Jake through the screen.

"Are you two having a private conversation out there, or can anybody join in?"

"I don't know, what'd you think?" Jake asked the dog. "You think we should let her in our club, or not?"

Otis cocked his head at Emma, letting out a muffled bark.

"Yeah, I guess you're right. After all, she does own the clubhouse." Looking over at Emma, Jake said, "Okay, I guess you're in."

"Thanks a lot. You two better watch your step, or you'll be holding your meetings out in the barn."

"Wouldn't be the first time," Jake muttered under his breath.

"What was that?"

"Oh, nothing. Looks like the steaks are done."

They settled down to a nice, quiet dinner. Now that they were coming to accept and trust each other, the need for small talk had vanished, and the ensuing periods of silence were no longer uncomfortable. After dinner, they had planned to continue their research, but the wine was making Emma light headed, and by the time the dishes were done it was nearly ten o'clock. Jake sat back down at the table and started to thumb through the notes from earlier in the day. He'd seemed somewhat tense ever since he'd returned to the house. The worried expression currently on his face had been there off and on all evening. She had the feeling more had happened to him during his trip to town than he was letting on. Her curiosity made her want to question him, but, Emma was sure that she would get no answer, at least not tonight. Taking another sip of wine, she knew that any in-depth discussions were going to have to wait until morning.

"Jake, I hope you don't mind, but, could we finish this tomorrow?"

Turning from the table, the frown lines in his forehead deepen. "I was really hoping that we might get a little further along tonight."

"I know you were, but, after half a bottle of wine, I'm not sure I'd be much help."

Jake's thoughts turned to the murdered corpse lying in a barn in Cedar Falls, and knew it was no coincidence, that it was connected to Emma. They needed to work fast to try to find out who was behind all of this. The time spent relaxing in each other's company had been wonderful, but, now the night had gotten away from them, and Jake realized Emma looked tired—beautiful, but tired. Knowing the smallest detail could be the exact clue they needed, and she would be able to think more clearly in the morning, he consented to call it quits for the evening.

"Okay. We'll get some sleep and make a fresh start in the morning."

"Thank you. I promise you'll have my undivided attention all day tomorrow."

"Don't worry about it. Sometimes you need to walk away from these things for a little while."

Stretching his long legs out in front of him, Jake leaned back in his chair and waited for Emma to make the next move. She was nervous, fidgeting with her wine glass, shuffling her feet, and glancing around the kitchen searching for the next thing she should say.

Her gaze returned to him. "I think I'll go take a hot bath."

"Sounds good. I think I'll take a hot shower myself."

Jake's face was unreadable. Emma had no doubt in her mind, however, that Jake had no intention of going back to his own cabin to take that shower.

"Well, I guess I'll see you in the morning then."

"Yeah. Good night."

Otis bumped into Jake's leg as he scrambled out from under the table to follow Emma out of the kitchen. The fact she hadn't asked him to lock up on his way out did not escape him. Jake was certain she was leaving the option open for him to, once again, stay the night. He watched her climb the stairs, and weighed his options, as he glanced at the upstairs hall—hot shower or, maybe, a hot bath. Reluctantly, he turned towards the downstairs guest room.

The stream of hot water beat down on the knots that had built up in Jake's neck and shoulders since earlier in the afternoon. For a full five minutes, he just stood under the pulsating shower head, as the welcomed heat penetrated his body, causing the tension in his muscles to begin to relax. A short while later, Jake stepped out of the shower, briskly drying off, and then slipped into a pair of navy blue sweat pants and a soft, grey T-shirt he had brought with him. As he entered the bedroom, the image of his feet hanging off the end of the small, double bed last night was more than Jake could handle. Emma's bedroom, on the other had, contained a large, comfy king bed. Walking out of the guest room, he secured all the doors and windows, turned out the lights, and headed for the stairs.

# Chapter Twenty

It was dark in the upstairs bath, except for several burning candles that were placed throughout the room. The window above the tub was open, and a breeze caused the flames to jump, creating dancing silhouettes on the walls. Emma sank down into the lavender scented bubble bath, which was hot enough to actually be somewhat uncomfortable when she first submerged herself into the water. As her skin became accustomed to the heat, she laid her head back on the blow-up pillow that was attached to the back of the tub by two little suction cups. Emma closed her eyes and allowed herself, for the first time today, the luxury of thinking about absolutely nothing. The fuzzy, tingling sensation that trickled through her body might have been due to the temperature of her bath, or the glasses of wine, or a combination of both. She didn't really know, or care. A soft, hush had filled the house ever since Emma had heard the downstairs shower shut off. It was apparent that Jake had no intention of leaving.

A drowsiness played at the corner of Emma's eyes, and her body began to relax. The world of dreams, which she always loved to wander through, beckoned to her. Yet, a small, nagging fear of unknown nightmares was stifling her ability to let herself drift away to places that could only be found in one's mind. The sound of a loud sigh reached her ears, as Otis readjusted himself on the floor, laying half in and half out of the bathroom door. A gentle smile appeared on Emma's face, and she reminded herself of just how safe she was. Unable to fight off the draining affects of the day any longer, she drifted off, never noticing Otis get up and leave, or the shadow that passed by the door.

Stepping out of the tub, she figured she must have been asleep at least twenty minutes, or so, due to how much the candles had burned down. Grabbing a big, fluffy purple towel off the hook by the shower, Emma dried herself off, and slipped into some emerald green, silk pajamas. She caught an image of herself in the bathroom mirror, as she brushed her teeth, and noticed the beginnings of dark circles that were starting to form under her eyes. The stress of the strange events over the past few days, and the return of the nightmares, were starting to take their toll. Running her fingers through her rich, brown curls, Emma turned away, blowing out the candles as she left.

"What took you so long? We've been waiting forever."

The husky voice coming out of the dark made Emma jump, when she reached around the edge of the door to flip up the wall switch that turned on the stained glass lamp sitting on her dresser. Both Jake and Otis were sprawled out on her bed, watching her.

"I *really* wish you would quit doing that! You're going to give me a heart attack one of these times."

Jake just smiled, and continued to rub Otis' neck and side, eliciting little sighs of contentment from the big retriever.

"Have you ever tried sleeping in that guest bed of yours?"

"No," Emma said. "Why?"

"Because the bottom two-thirds of the mattress is missing."

Jake replied, adjusting himself into a sitting position with his back against the wall.

"Is that so." Emma walked around the king bed. Otis leisurely rolled himself across the top, meeting her on the far side. She kissed the top of his furry head before he scrambled off the bed.

"Yeah, that's so. My feet hang off the end, which makes my toes cold."

Emma couldn't help but laugh a little, at the image of Jake's feet sticking out from under the burgundy comforter.

"So, what do you propose to do about it?" she asked with a mischievous twinkle in her eye.

"I propose to sleep up here tonight, and I promise to be good."

"Hmm. I don't know if that's such a good idea. I mean, I barely know you."

"Look, I have my clothes on, and I'll even sleep on top of the covers, if that makes you feel better."

"Won't your toes still get cold?" Emma gave him a mock look of sympathy.

"Yeah, but, it's better than nearly falling off the bed every time I turn over."

Crossing her arms over her chest, Emma studied Jake. It amazed her how someone so solid and strong, could also have such a rumpled, boyish charm about him. Right now, with his bare feet and uncombed hair, he was very appealing. Dropping her eyes to Otis, who was sitting by her feet, head on the edge of the mattress, she felt confident that she was making the right decision.

"Okay, you can stay," Emma said, lifting up the comforter and slipping under the sheet.

"Thank you." Jake, keeping his word, stretched out on the top of the bed.

They laid that way, saying nothing, for several minutes. Emma finally broke the silence.

"You can sleep under the covers, if you want."

"I was hoping you'd say that." Jake jumped up and quickly climbed in on his side.

"Well, I don't want to be responsible for you having frozen toes in the morning."

"Thanks." Realizing he had not turned the light off, Jake started to rise.

"Don't get up." Emma said. "Otis, lights."

The dog walked over to the door and jumped up, placing his front paws gently on the wall. Otis slid his right paw down over the flat light switch, turning off the lamp. The bright, full harvest moon sent sparkling shafts of light through the window, bathing the room in a soft, silvery glow.

"Nifty trick," Jake said with admiration.

"It comes in handy, especially in the winter, when I'm all snuggled up in my comforter, and don't want to get back up," Emma explained, turning on her side to face him lying next to her in the shadows.

"Jake?"

"Hmm." His voice sounded sleepy.

"I'm really glad you're here."

Jake rolled over, propping himself up on his elbow. Pushing back a stray curl from her forehead, he let his fingers trace the contours of her cheekbones and chin, coming to rest on her lips. Leaning down, he placed small kisses on her forehead, the tip of her nose, and her sensuous mouth. He could feel her move closer to him. Emma reached up, pulling his head towards her, searching to find his lips with hers. Her body trembled with the intimacy that had escaped her all these many years. She wanted so badly to feel his body against hers, but, was wary of moving too fast.

Jake felt Emma's lips move tentatively under his. She tasted so sweet. Their bodies were now touching, and Jake increased the pressure of his kisses. He traced the outline of her lips with his tongue, delving into the warmth of her mouth, claiming Emma for his own. She had slipped her arms around his neck, to start, but, now her fingers were tracing the muscles along his back. Heat was building up between them. Even clothing couldn't keep the electricity from jumping back and forth, setting their emotions and bodies on fire, and Emma could feel Jake's rising desire against her stomach.

Jake moved his hand along the silky material covering Emma's hip and then explored under her camisole. Her skin felt cool and sleek. Kissing her more passionately, he cupped her breast, marveling at how it felt in his hand. Gently, he rubbed her nipple with this thumb, bring it to a perfect peak. Although Emma let out a soft groan, Jake felt a sudden tension in her body. Breaking their kiss, he tried to read what was in her deep, green eyes.

"Why did you stop?" Emma mumbled, her voice and eyes still full of the desire she was feeling just moments before.

"Em, are you sure you want to do this?"

Her first impulse was to say yes, to tell him she had never wanted anything as much as she wanted him right now. Jake's silver eyes were now several shades darker with desire, but, Emma could read in them his concern for her. She knew he would be fine with whatever her answer was. Reaching up, she laid her hand on the side of his face, letting her fingers drift through the hair at his temple.

"Thank you, Jake."

"For what?"

"For asking me what I want?"

The look of gratitude on Emma's face surprised him.

"Why wouldn't I ask you? This affects you, too, you know." Jake gave her a quick kiss on her nose.

"I guess I just wasn't used to that from a man."

Understanding where she was coming from, Jake merely caressed her face, and remained silent.

"I would like it if we could just lay here together, and hold each other. Okay?"

Reaching around her, he grabbed the comforter, which they had previously kicked off the bottom of the bed, and covered them both up. Snuggling up against his shoulder, Emma starting rubbing her fingers over his chest. Jake loved the way she smelled, the warmth of her, and he could feel himself relaxing under her feather like touch. He was just thinking there was no other place he would rather be, when the bed shook and a hundred-pound weight fell on top of his feet. Staring down at the end of the bed, he could see Otis. Well, he couldn't really see the dog, but, a pair of reflective, green eyes stared at him from out of the dark. Jake could hear Emma stifling a laugh next to him.

"He usually sleeps with me," she explained. "I'm sure he's just as surprised to see you, as you are to see him."

"Well, this bed ain't big enough for the three of us, so somebody has to go."

"Let's see. You're my guest, and I just don't have the heart to kick him off, so I guess the only solution is for me to go," Emma said jokingly, as she rolled toward the edge of the bed.

"I don't think so." Grabbing her from behind, Jake pulled her close. "It won't hurt him to spend a night on the floor, like other dogs do."

"Problem is, he doesn't think he's a dog."

"Well, what's that they say, 'You learn something new every day.' Guess he's going to learn something new."

Nudging Otis with his foot, and in a voice that let the dog

know who was going to win this battle, Jake said, "All right, buddy, on the floor."

The bed rocked as Otis, with obvious reluctance, climbed down, collapsing on the floor beside Jake with a big sigh of rejection. Jake reached over the side of the bed, petting the big dog.

"You're a good boy," Jake said, and was answered by a tail thumping on the floor.

Rolling over, Jake gathered Emma up in his arms. "Now, isn't this better?"

"It's perfect," she answered him. "Absolutely, perfect."

# Chapter Twenty-One

The dream came to her for the second night in a row, once more taking a different turn. She was again overpowered by the smell of something sweet, something she should know. The face Emma had seen reflected in the mirror was there also, yet, this time it was as she passed by the fireplace. It appeared to her in the glass of the picture hanging above the mantel, but, the features blended in with the painting, so she still couldn't see who it was. Knowing she would find no one there, Emma still turned around finding the room empty. Her focus returned to the body. To move the few feet from the fireplace to the bed seemed to take forever, as it does in dreams. Reaching out to touch him, Emma noticed the violent shaking in her hands. After all the times of having this dream, she'd never felt as scared as she did right now. She tried, in vain, to wake herself up from the nightmare, but its grip was too tight. Emma knew, more than ever, she did not want to turn him over this time, however, she was unable to stop herself. Taking a deep breath, Emma turned the body over, and found herself staring at Jake's face.

Jake's deep sleep was shattered by Emma screaming his name. She was sitting up, her body shaking in uncontrollable tremors, as tears ran down her face. Pulling her down to him, he cocooned her in his arms, gently forcing her into the soft curve of his shoulder. Kissing the top of her head, Jake continued to whisper reassuring words to her, all the while stroking her body until her shaking started to subside. After it became apparent that Emma had stopped crying, he tilted her head back so he could see her face. The terror was still fresh in her eyes, and it pained him that he could not save her from her own dreams.

"Do you want to tell me about it?" His voice was quiet and soothing.

Emma looked at his strong, handsome face, not knowing how she could ever tell him what she had dreamed. Turning her face away, she shook her head no.

"Em, you'll feel better if you do. You know you will."

She knew what he really meant was that he'd feel better if he knew what she was thinking. She could only hope what she'd dreamed was just that, a dream, and not a premonition of things to come. But, if it was, Emma knew he had a right to know.

"It was you." Her words were so soft, he almost didn't hear them.

"What was me?"

"The body in my dream. When I rolled it over this time, it wasn't Charles, it was you." Turning back to face him, she tried to fight back the tears that were once again forming in her eyes.

Engulfing her in his arms, Jake began rubbing up and down her back. "Nothing's going to happen to me. It was just a dream." She didn't say anything, and he could still feel the tension that had possessed her body. "You know it was just a dream, don't you?"

Emma nodded her head, but, he knew she wasn't totally convinced.

"Everything's going to be all right, Em. I promise you."

Lifting her head towards him, she gave him a tentative smile. The dream's affects were going to take a while to wear off.

"How about we get up, and I'll make us some breakfast?"

Emma brushed Jake's hair back away from his face. Continuing to let her fingers trail through his dark, wavy hair, she gave him a long, lingering kiss. Her kiss was the kind that told him now, in no uncertain terms, what was in her heart. At that point, Jake realized how much she wanted him, not only in her bed, but in her life as well.

"Thank you," she said.

"For what?"

"For being here."

"No place in the world I'd rather be."

This time the smile she gave him was no longer sad, and it came from her heart. He returned her smile with a heartfelt one of his own.

"So, you want that breakfast?"

"Yeah. I'll make the coffee."

As Jake started to roll out of bed, he became conscience, for the first time since waking up, of the heavy weight on his feet. Before he even looked, he knew what was there. Otis was stretched out across the foot of the bed, front paws crossed, head cocked, watching them.

"I thought I told you to sleep on the floor." The dog's only answer was to cock his head the other way. "He doesn't listen very well, does he?"

"Oh, he listens. He just doesn't pay any attention."

"Hmm."

"Well, after all you did sort of move in on his job."

"His job?"

"Sure. Until you came along, he was my only protection, and he was pretty serious about that, you know."

"I see." Jake leaned forward and ruffled the big dog's ears. "I guess you and I are going to have to work together from now on."

Emma's heart swelled, as she realized that she now had two protectors in her life.

After a late breakfast, Jake headed back to his cabin. Emma had wanted to go with him, but he'd convinced her to stay, telling her he needed her to concentrate on continuing to put together additional information regarding Charles. In truth, he didn't want her to see all the surveillance equipment at the cabin before he had a chance to tell her about it. Otis had also tried to follow him, but, Jake had sent him back home, feeling more comfortable with the dog being there when he couldn't be.

Upon arriving at the cabin, Jake turned on the monitor first thing, so he could keep a constant eye on Emma. Rewinding the tape from the previous night, he took it out of the recording unit, putting into another VCR hooked up to the TV. The outside cameras showed that nothing appeared to be out of the ordinary, which made him feel a little better. Maybe whoever had been watching Emma decided to leave when they discovered he was becoming a more permanent fixture around the place. Jake thought perhaps he should just go ahead and tell Emma about the surveillance equipment, and move it all to her house. It no longer made sense for him to have to keep coming back to the cabin every day. Besides, he could protect her better at her own home, and that's where he wanted to be anyway. Jake made up his mind he would come clean with her tonight. Suspecting she would initially be angry, he was pretty certain he could convince her that his spying on her had been for her own good.

Jake sat down at the table and started re-reading the file he had on Charles' murder. The police had been in the middle of an in-depth study into Charles' past, right before the investigation came to an abrupt halt. He was hoping to find some common denominator between what was in the police file, and what he and Emma were coming up with. Both of them were now convinced that it had not been a burglar. The fact that the body, and most importantly the face, had been mutilated almost beyond recognition, made it something much more personal. In Jake's experience, a crime of passion, such as this, almost always left some kind of clue as to who the murderer might be—he just needed to find it.

As Jake continued to study the file, he kept an eye on Emma as she wandered aimlessly around the house. Once or twice, she sat down at the kitchen table and tried to work on the notes he had left for her, but, her mind wasn't on the task at hand. Moving into the living room, Emma called Henry, who, from what Jake could tell from one side of the conversation, provided her with some work to do. For the next hour or so, as he finished up his research, he could hear her typing at the computer. It was late in the afternoon, when Jake closed the file and put it away. Checking the monitor, he watched Emma enter the kitchen. She made the rounds of the cupboards, pantry, and refrigerator, looking somewhat perplexed by the time she was through.

"What'd you think he'd like for dinner?" Emma asked Otis. "You think he's a pizza kind of guy?" Otis began turning little circles in front of her, wagging his tail. "Yeah, I know you like pizza. How about we call Pizza To Go?" Otis barked in agreement.

Emma leafed through the phone book, finding an ad for the restaurant in the yellow pages. Seeing the phone number, Emma shook her head in exasperation.

"Why in the world do they have to use letters in the phone number? It's a pain in the butt to have to try to figure it out. Let's see, "togo" would be 8646."

Emma called the pizza place, conversing with the dog first

trying to figure out what kind of pizza to get. It was no surprise that Otis' vote was all meat, but, Emma's was vegetarian, so she settled on a deluxe combo which she figured should make all of them happy. Jake liked the fact that she was obviously anticipating his return. After hanging up, Emma sat down cross-legged on the floor, so that she was now eye-to-eye with the dog.

"So, tell me, what do you think of our new friend?" The dog looked at her with a curious expression. "I know he's handsome, boy is he handsome, and he's kind of funny. He's also been really kind and thoughtful, all the things you always want in someone." Taking Otis' face between her hands, she asked the dog, "Do you think I'm letting myself in for heartache again? After all, I thought Charles had a lot of good qualities, until after we got married."

Otis' gaze was steady as he looked her in the eye. Again, she felt as if he was reading her mind, feeling her every emotion.

"You like him, don't you?" Otis' bark was confident. "You trust him, too, don't you?" She received the same answer. "Well, you've never steered me wrong yet. Besides, I think I'm falling in love with him. But don't you tell him that." Otis gave her a little doggie kiss on the cheek, and nuzzled his head under her chin. Emma grinned, laying her head against the fluffy fur of his neck, hugging him tight.

Thousands of butterflies fluttered about in Jake's stomach, as Emma's words filled his ears. He'd tried to stay professional, but, it had been impossible. From the minute he saw her, he knew he would wind up falling in love with her, and now he knew she felt the same. Keeping her safe now became even more important, because Jake knew she would always be a part of his life.

Putting a new tape in the machine, Jake double checked the equipment before getting ready to leave. On the way out the door, the laptop computer caught his attention, and he realized he hadn't checked for messages since returning to the cabin. More than likely there wasn't anything too pressing, but, he decided he'd better to check them anyway. Switching on the computer, Jake waited the few seconds for the screen to come into focus, and then selected the e-mail icon. There were three messages, one of them from his anonymous client. Double clicking on the message, the blood drained from Jake's face as he read the message that appeared in front of him. Falling back into the ladder-back chair, Jake could only continue to stare at the words that were filling up the computer screen.

> *Dear Mr. McLean:*
>
> *I apologize for not getting back to you sooner, as I have been rather busy. I had anticipated this change in plans, for I, myself, know how irresistible Emma can be. However, it is unfortunate that you have become this deeply involved, as there is no way that you will be able to prevent Emma's pending death, or your own. The game is quickly coming to an end and, as before, I will win. However, for sport, I shall provide you with a clue to my identity. It has been right before your eyes every time I contacted you, and the solution is at your fingertips. Good luck!*

Jake knew that he should return to Emma's as quick as possible, but, he felt cemented to the chair. The fact that he now realized he'd been working for Charles' murderer all along, made him sick to his stomach. His reports had kept them abreast of Emma's every move, providing them with very detailed and personalized information. They'd been hoping Jake would tell them if Emma remembered anything about the night of Charles' death that would lead back to them. Learning of Emma's recurring nightmares only after he had quit, had been a blessing in disguise, making him very grateful. However, Jake knew that time was running out. Reading the message again, he found it strange they now wanted to give him a clue as to who they were. He had to get back to Emma right away. She needed, more than ever now, to try to remember anything she could of Charles' past.

Jake clicked on the print button, and heard the printer kick in as it spit out a hard copy of the message. While trying to decide whether to save the message or delete it, he noticed the little, pink sticky note he had attached to the top, right corner of the computer screen. On it were the numbers he had copied down from Emma's address book. Something about those particular numbers seemed so familiar. He knew he had seen that sequence before. Examining his anonymous client's e-mail address more closely, Jake noticed it was all numbers. Pulling the piece of paper off the top of the computer, he held it up beside the numbers on the message. They didn't match, but, Jake's subconscious told him to continue to look harder. He was concentrating so hard on the two sets of numbers, that after a while it seemed as if they were blurring into one. After resting his eyes for moment, Jake returned his focus to the screen, and the answer seem to come to him from out of nowhere. The numbers in the e-mail, he realized, were the exact reversal of the numbers he'd found at Emma's. Whoever had hired him, was also corresponding with Emma, and it was becoming a matter of life and death that he find out who it was. Calling in a favor from his friends at the Marshal's Service to trace the e-mail address could take days, and he knew without a doubt they didn't have that kind of time. The most logical step was to ask Emma, however, Jake's suspicious nature made him wonder if this person would've let Emma know who they were. They'd been playing a game with him, so it made sense they could be playing a game with her, too.

He was about to shut down the computer and secure the cabin, when Emma's words from a little bit ago came back to him.

She had been ticked off with having to decipher the phone number to the pizza place. Could the numbers in the e-mail addresses correspond to letters in the alphabet? That seemed too simple, however, after Jake thought more about it, it was becoming evident that this sick, perverted person wanted him to find out who they were. Sitting back down, Jake first considered comparing the numbers to their corresponding letter in the alphabet, but, with twenty-six letters it was unlikely that was the solution. Next he used the corresponding numbers and letters on the phone, as Emma had done, trying to come up with a name that would be familiar. After nearly a half an hour, Jake was no further ahead. He was getting angrier by the minute at not being able to break the code. The numbers had to mean something, and the later it got, the more frightened he was for Emma. The answer had to be there in front of him. Frustrated, rubbing his forehead, Jake stared down at the laptop in front of him. Shafts of broken sunlight made their way through the kitchen window, reflecting off the keyboard, as the sun started to sink in the sky. Watching the red light flicker along the keys, Jake became aware of how the letters lined up diagonally under the number keys on the top row. Then the words from his client's final message rang in his head, "It has been right before your eyes every time I contacted you, and the solution is at your fingertips." Encouraged, Jake spent the next forty-five minutes arranging and rearranging letters until a name began to take shape, a name he had seen before. He had to get to Emma.

# Chapter Twenty-Two

Lieutenant Harris' day had not gone well. After being in court most of the afternoon regarding a sexual assault case where the perpetrator had been allowed to walk due to a technical failure on the part of the District Attorney's office, all Harris wanted to do was go home. The phone call currently ringing through to his desk was an unwelcome, last minute intrusion. The clock on the wall above the door showed that he had only ten minutes remaining on his shift. Harris knew if he didn't answer it, the call would go back to the operator and be assigned to someone else. Unfortunately, Harris' extreme sense of duty, and the thought of his lonely one bedroom apartment, wouldn't allow him to do that, and he snatched the handset from its cradle.

"Harris, here." He tried to keep the irritation from his voice, but, didn't completely succeed.

"Lieutenant Harris, this is Katherine Werner. Am I disturbing you?"

The voice on the other end took Harris by surprise. Miss Werner was the woman who had bought Emma Hudson's house after the murder. He had paid her a visit shortly after she had moved in, asking that she let him know if she discovered anything that might help him with the case. Harris, however, had never really expected to hear from her.

"Miss Werner, you're not disturbing me at all. What can I do for you?"

"I think it's more like what I can for you, Lieutenant. Would you be able to come by the house right now?"

"Certainly. But, what's this all about?"

"There's something here I really think you need to see, and I don't want to touch anything until you get here."

"Does it have to do with the Hudson murder?"

"I believe so."

"I'll be right there."

\* \* \*

Harris pulled up in front of the formidable stone house. Not much had changed on the outside. He punched the door bell, and heard the sound of elegant chimes echoing in the front hall. Almost immediately, the front door was answered by a tall, stately woman. Katherine Werner was approximately 50 years old, slender, with short, sandy blonde hair. She was impeccably dressed in jade green slacks, and a cream-colored silk blouse.

"Thank you for coming, Lieutenant. Please come in." Katherine's warm voice and welcoming smile seemed in contrast to her perfect appearance.

The inside of the home had definitely changed since the Hudsons lived here. Although the outside still had a cold, dreary feeling, Katherine's personal touches had added light and warmth to all the rooms in the house.

"I really like what you've done with the place," Harris commented

"Thank you. I knew there was a lot of potential here."

"Are you still remodeling?"

"Yes. Actually, that's why I called you. I want to show you what my contractor found in the master bedroom."

Katherine lead Harris up the front staircase. The dark Persian hallway rug had been removed, and beautiful white marble tiles laced with silver-blue swirls took its place. Upon entering the bedroom, Harris couldn't believe he was in the same room that he had stood in almost a year ago. Gone was all the dark furniture, replaced by antique cherry wood dressers, chairs and a desk. The draperies and bedding had been redone in soft shades of peaches and greens. Harris looked around approvingly, knowing that Emma would have loved all these changes.

"What I wanted to show you is over here in the closet," Katherine said. "You probably remember that originally there were two closets, a his and a hers. Since I have no need for a his, I just decided to make myself one big hers."

Harris couldn't help but smile at Katherine's comment, as he followed her into the "his" closet.

"My contractor was pulling out the built-in shelves and came across this." Katherine had stopped in front of an open door. "We didn't touch anything inside, but, I think your Mr. Hudson may have been somewhat of a voyeur. I left the light on for you."

Harris stepped across the threshold into the enclosed room. The walls were lined with video tapes. The only thing written on the labels were various dates. A television set with a VCR player connected to it, sat on a small table in front of a recliner. At the end of the room, where the wall was common with the bedroom, was a shelf about three quarters of the way up the wall. A video camera sat on the shelf facing the wall, its lens seeming to melt into the paneling. Harris walked back out into the bedroom to look at the wall between the two closets. The only thing there was a smoke detector. Although Katherine's arrangement of her furniture was different than when Emma owned the place, Harris knew at the time of the murder that the camera would have been directly in line with the bed.

"I'm assuming that this smoke detector would have been of little use to me, if I had had a fire. Is that right?" Katherine asked, while studying the alarm.

"I'm pretty sure the only thing it could have done was record the fire," Harris responded.

"If neither Mrs. Hudson, nor Mr. Hudson's murderer, was aware of the camera, do you suppose there's still a tape in it?"

Harris met Katherine's steady gaze, then returned to the video room. Slipping on a pair of latex gloves, he punched the eject button on the camera, and was rewarded with a tape. He turned on the television and VCR, inserting the tape into the slot. A remote control sat on top of the recording unit. Picking it up, Harris sat on the very edge of the recliner, and hit the rewind button. A soft, audible, click indicated that the tape was back to the beginning, and ready for play. Harris glanced at Katherine, who was standing in the doorway.

"Are you sure you want to see this?" Harris asked her.

"If it's part of your investigation, and you would rather I didn't, I can leave," Katherine said, though she made no move to do so.

"Technically, the case is closed. I've been working on it on my own time, so, there's nothing privileged about the info at this time. Besides, it's your house."

"Then I think I'll stay."

Harris had to admit that he liked this strong, attractive woman. Giving her a slight smile, and nod, he turned back to the television and hit the play button. As the images of the murder filled the screen, Harris felt a sinking sensation in this stomach.

"Oh, my God!" Harris exclaimed, as the killer's face became quite clear on the screen.

"Do you know that person?" Katherine asked, even though the look on Harris' face had already given her the answer to that question.

"Yeah," Harris replied, flipping open his cell phone and punching a button.

"Calling the police?"

"No, Emma." The phone rang and rang and rang, with no answer, not even Emma's machine picked up the call.

"Damn, it!" Harris said, as he punched in another number and hit send.

"Are you calling the police this time?" Katherine inquired.

"Yeah, the Cedar Falls Sheriff's office."

# Chapter Twenty-Three

Matt sat at the counter in the Cedar Falls Café, as he did almost every evening, totally unaware of the eyes that watched him from a booth in the back. His full attention was focused on Maggie who, in her usual light hearted manner, was waiting on tonight's customary dinner crowd. Maggie's father was the café's cook, and had a county-wide reputation for making the best chicken fried steak in the area, which had been Monday night's special since the place had opened. Because of this, the café was filled on what typically would be a slow night for most restaurants. Maggie always choose to work the counter—so she could be sure to wait on Matt—along with a couple of tables, while Janet, a short, stocky woman with graying hair, serviced all the booths. That was the main reason why the eyes had made a specific point to be seated in one of those booths. They had felt extremely uncomfortable the last time Maggie had waited on them. The waitress had a strength and confidence about her that made them uneasy, and they suspected that the dazzling redhead was suspicious of them. If it wasn't for the fact that it had become very important to keep tabs on the deputy, ever since the body had been found, they would have never set foot inside the café again.

They now followed Maggie from across the room, as she brought the deputy his dinner.

"Dad's wonderin' why you didn't order his chicken fried steak?" Maggie asked, putting a large chef's salad down on the counter.

"Just thought I'd try somethin' different for a change."

"Yeah, but a chef's salad? I thought you law enforcement guys needed to keep your strength up."

"The only thing that's been going up is my weight. I don't get much exercise ridin' around in a car all day. Thought it couldn't hurt to lose a couple of pounds, get back in shape, ya know?"

"So, what brought all this on?"

"Nothin'," Matt said, looking a little sheepish. "Can't a man just want to look good?"

"Well, sure. But, ya know," Maggie said over her shoulder as she headed down the counter, "I like a little meat on my men."

Matt looked down at the salad, then back at Maggie, who was now chatting with an older couple who were Monday night regulars. Sliding him a sideways glance, she gave Matt a wink and a saucy smile. He grinned at her, then returning his attention to the salad, he simply shrugged, picked up his fork, and began eating. A couple of minutes later, while Matt was in mid-bite, a perfect, manicured hand removed the salad in front of him replacing it with chicken fried steak, mashed potatoes, and luscious cream gravy. Surprised, he looked up into a pair of twinkling, mischievous eyes.

"Trust me, I know what's good for you."

"I'll bet you do."

About half way through his dinner, the pager on Matt's belt tingled against his side. It had been his night off, and he had selected the vibrate position, so as not to disturb the restaurant's patrons. Unclipping the pager from his belt, Matt read the message. Both Maggie and the eyes watched him when he got up and used the phone behind the counter to call in. Assuming it was Sheriff Henderson that Matt was talking to, Maggie watched his expression change from curious to worried. Hanging up the phone, Matt headed straight toward the cash register and Maggie met him there. Reaching in his pocket, he pulled out his silver money clip.

"Gotta go, Maggie. How much do I owe ya?"

"Never mind about that, is everything okay?" Concern tinted the beautiful features of her face.

"I've got to get out to Emma's place."

"Is she all right?" A tinge of panic started to creep into Maggie voice, as images of the dark haired stranger flashed through her mind. If he'd had done anything to Emma, and she hadn't told the police about him, she'd never forgive herself.

"Yeah, I'm sure she's okay, but, they identified the body that was found in the coffin at the Taylor's place. Turns out it was a friend of Emma's. Mike asked me to go talk to her."

Maggie started to tell Matt about the man he might find out there, but, for some reason that she'll never understand, she didn't. All she said was, "Matt, just be really careful."

Smiling at her, he replied, "I'm always careful."

Then, much to her surprise, he leaned over the cash register, giving her a quick kiss on the lips before heading out the door. Stunned by Matt's unexpected show of affection, Maggie almost missed seeing the mysterious stranger once again follow him out. She hadn't paid any particular attention to that customer all evening, but had been aware of them from the moment they had entered the restaurant. Recognizing them as the same person who had followed Matt out of the café yesterday, her woman's intuition told her something was very wrong. The stranger had been at the counter paying their bill, and within easy earshot to hear Matt's conversation. Maggie sensed that Matt was headed for big trouble. Looking around, she realized there wasn't a single empty table in the entire place. This wasn't going to be a good time for her to leave, but, Maggie knew, without a doubt, if she didn't Matt just might not survive the night. Untying her apron, she stashed it under the counter. Sticking her head through the window between the dining room and kitchen, she caught her father's attention.

"Dad, I'm sorry to do this to you, but, somethin's come up, and I've really gotta go."

"Maggie, darlin', we're swamped out there tonight. Janet can't handle it all herself."

"She gonna have to. I wouldn't leave unless it was really important."

"What could be that important, Maggie?" Her father was starting to sound irritated.

"It may literally be a matter of life and death."

"Oh? Who's?"

"Matt's." There was no question from look she gave her father Maggie was serious about what she was telling him. Without another word, he nodded his head in understanding.

Calling Janet over, Maggie explained she had to leave. Reaching under the register to get the truck keys, her hand brushed up against the cold steel of a 9mm handgun. It was kept there in the unlikely event that they were ever robbed. Something told her that tonight she just might need it. Grabbing the gun, Maggie tucked it in her jeans, threw on her sweater, and headed out the door, hoping she wasn't too late.

\* \* \*

The eyes had beat the deputy out of town, and had set up a diversion along the two lane road leading out to Emma's house.

Unlike the roads in many other states, Missouri's secondary roads were narrow, winding, and demanded your undivided attention. Very few had any kind of shoulder, so if a car broke down there would be a good chance it would wind up in the middle of the road. The eyes had parked their car in one of the few straightaways between town and Emma's house. Darkness had fallen, so they had turned on the flashers, wanting to make sure that the deputy would see them and stop. As they waited for him, they started to think about how he had kissed the waitress before he left. Emma would have been crushed if she had known what was going on behind her back. It was a repeat of how Charles had treated her, and no one was going to hurt her again like that. The longer they sat there, the more the eyes filled with hatred. Eliminating the deputy would be the only way to quell the immediate fire that burned in their depths.

\* \* \*

On the drive to Emma's, Matt tried to figure out how he was going to break the news to her. Emma had never expounded on her life in Colorado, however, she had, on a number of occasions, talked about two or three friends that she still had with whom she remained quite close. Now, he was going to have the unfortunate task of telling her one of them was dead. What bothered him the most was he was sure she would want to know how they died, and Matt didn't want to have to describe to her the image that had been imprinted on his brain from yesterday's discovery. The investigation was still ongoing, and because of that there would be many of her questions he was not going to be able to answer right now.

Matt first spotted the car when he came around a bend in the road. It was stopped just short of the bridge that went over No

Name Creek. He'd lived here all his life, and still had to chuckle at the creek's name. Rumor was that when the state surveyors came to map out the area, all the locals told them that no one had ever bothered to name the creek, so in the official records it was listed as "No Name Creek". Coming up from behind, the police cruiser's headlights reflected off a nondescript, white car parked in the lane ahead. Matt could make out a figure kneeling down beside the back tire on the driver's side. Irritated, because he wanted to get out to Emma's before it got too late, Matt was grumbling to himself as he stopped the cruiser a few feet behind the disabled sedan. Pulling himself together, he knew he couldn't let personal feelings interfere with helping a stranded motorist, especially not one out here in the middle of nowhere. Shutting off the engine, Matt flipped on the overhead beacons and stepped out of his patrol car.

\* \* \*

Maggie knew these mountain roads like the back of her hand. She also knew that driving too fast on them in the dark was not only dangerous, but, was something no intelligent person would do. Tonight, however, her emotions were overriding her logic, and she took each corner and hill with nothing more than blind faith that nothing would be on the other side. She had to get to Matt before he got to Emma's. Thick, gray thunderclouds were rolling in, shutting out any light that might have been had from the moon. The air had become heavy and still, and the surrounding darkness seemed ominous. Maggie looked out at the Ozark hills that she had always loved, and noticed that tonight the shadows created from her headlights hitting the trees, seemed eerie.

Rounding the bend that was right before No Name Creek,

Maggie felt relieved when she spotted the red and blue rotating lights on the top of Matt's cruiser. Now that she'd caught up with him, everything would be fine. Matt was just stepping out of his vehicle, walking around the open door heading towards the car in front of him. Slowing down as she approached the two vehicles, Maggie intended to pull in behind the patrol car. All at once, a small, red fox came scurrying out of the woods on the right, stopping in the lane ahead of her. In an attempt to avoid hitting the animal, Maggie was forced over into the oncoming lane. The truck's headlights, which had yet to be dimmed, illuminated the entire area around the two vehicles ahead of her. The lone motorist had stood up, and was turning toward the deputy. It took only seconds for Maggie to realize there was gun in the person's hand, and it was aimed precisely at Matt's chest. As she maneuvered back into the right lane, the truck's bright lights hit the assailant straight on, blinding them just as they squeezed the trigger.

The world dissolved into slow motion as Maggie watched Matt grab his left leg right above the knee, and sink to the ground. An uncontrollable anger overwhelmed her. Without a second thought to her own safety, Maggie slammed on the brakes, threw the truck in park, and jumped out. Whipping the semi-automatic pistol out of her jeans, she started shooting at the figure standing by the car. Startled by the fact that this woman had a gun, and had also chosen to use it, the figure fled to the open driver's door. Jumping in, they wasted no time in revving up the engine, spraying gravel as they hightailed it down the road. Maggie continued firing, emptying the gun at the retreating car. The sound of shattering glass echoed off the dark walls of the forest. Since both of the car's taillights were still visible, Maggie assumed that one of her bullets had made contact with the back window.

Dropping the gun, she turned and ran to where Matt lay next

to the front bumper of the cruiser. He was alive and conscious, but, the wound appeared to be serious. Afraid that perhaps an artery had been severed, due to the amount of blood on the ground, Maggie took off her belt and placed it around Matt's leg, instructing him to hold it tight. Once she was certain that he could manage, she got on the radio and called into the station.

"Sherry, come in Sherry, it's Maggie. Matt's been shot and we need an ambulance out here on Route 3." Up to this point, Maggie's anger had kept her somewhat calm, but, now fear for Matt's life caused her voice to shake. "And, you also better tell Mike to get someone out to Emma Hudson's as fast as he can, I think there's gonna be trouble."

"Yeah, we know. Just got a call from a detective in Denver, who knows who killed Emma's husband." Sherry's voice crackled back over the two-way. "Did you see who shot Matt?"

Peering down the road into what seemed like an endless tunnel of evil blackness, Maggie answered, "No, but, I can tell you whoever it was is on their way to Emma's."

# Chapter Twenty-Four

The delicious aroma of sausage and mushroom pizza hit Jake full force as he entered Emma's back door. She was at the kitchen table, beer in hand, Otis at her feet, reviewing the notes from their previous session. Leaning back in the chair, she gave him a mock look of annoyance.

"Hey, where have you been? We were about to start without you."

"Sorry, I'm late."

"You're just lucky that we're polite. We had to discuss whether you were even a pizza kind of guy to begin with, and then guess at what kind of pizza you might like."

"Yeah, I know."

"You know?" A quizzical expression passed across Emma's face.

Ignoring it, Jake said, "Never mind, I'll explain later. Em, I know who killed Charles, and who's been stalking you."

"You do?"

"Yeah. I don't know why it didn't come to me sooner. I feel so stupid. I was actually working for the guy."

"Are you talking about your anonymous client?"

"He's not anonymous anymore. He sent me an e-mail message today, and a not very nice one at that."

Taking a piece of paper out of his pocket, he unfolded it, tossing the hard copy of the e-mail on the table in front of Emma. The muscles in her stomach tightened and her heart began to race as the meaning of the note became clear to her.

"Who is it, Jake?"

"David Meyers."

Emma's eyes widened in disbelief. "David? You've got to be kidding. He's one of my closest friends."

"I think he wants to be more than friends."

"No." Emma shook her head. "You've gotta be wrong. He'd never hurt me."

"Look, Em, I know I'm right. It all makes sense. He was jealous of Charles because he wanted you for himself. When you didn't come running to him after Charles' death, you probably broke the guy's heart. He may have started wondering if you knew more about Charles' death than you were letting on."

"I don't know, Jake. How can you be so sure?"

Excited, Jake started to pace around the kitchen, telling Emma what he had figured out that afternoon.

"I was staring at the screen, reading the message over and over, trying to figure out the clue. Then, I noticed the note with the numbers I had found in your address book the other day."

"My address book?" Emma frowned, an edginess was beginning to creep into her voice.

"The numbers from your book were the exact reversal of the numbers for the e-mail address of my client. I was sure that they must mean something. Then I remembered what you said."

"What I said?"

"Yeah. I saw how pissed off you got when you had to translate the Pizza To Go phone number from letters to numbers. It got me thinking that maybe these numbers could be translated back to letters. I tried using the phone pad first, but, I wasn't getting anywhere." The icy silence that was filling up the kitchen completely escaped Jake's attention. "I was really getting frustrated, and was just sitting there staring at the computer, when all of sudden it hit me. I noticed how the letters on the keyboard lined up in a diagonal row under the top row of number keys. It took me a little while of experimenting, but, I came up with David's name." Turning to look at Emma, Jake gave her a cocky smile. "But, as smart as I might be, I couldn't have done it without you."

The reaction Jake had expected from Emma was definitely not the one he was getting now, and his smile started to fade. She was standing behind her chair, stiff and unmoving, arms crossed in front of her, her face expressionless. It was almost like she had turned to stone, except for a hot blaze that was burning in her vivid, green eyes. Jake was sure if she continued to look at him that way much longer he would soon be reduced to a pile of smoldering ashes. Why was she so angry? Shouldn't she be happy that they had not only found out who their adversary was, but, that she had played a big part in it? If he hadn't overheard Emma's phone call to the pizza place, it might have taken him a lot longer to figure things out. Panic hit Jake like a tidal wave, as the realization of all he had told her set in. Without ever meaning to, he had let her know all that he had been hiding from her. He took a cautious step toward her.

"Emma?" His voice was unsteady.

"You've been spying on me, haven't you?" Her words were soft and deliberate, but, the underlying anger in her voice was unmistakable.

"I was just trying to protect you."

"By invading my privacy? What, you have bugs or something planted all over my house?"

"Some."

Caught off guard by his answer, she paused a moment. "You said you 'saw' how pissed off I was. You have more than just listening devices in here, don't you?"

Swallowing hard, Jake's silver eyes met hers with a mixture of guilt and sadness. This wasn't the way he had wanted her to find out. Taking a deep breath, he answered her, "Yeah, there's a couple of cameras in here, too."

For what seemed like an eternity, Emma said nothing. She was trying to remain emotionless, but, Jake could see a shimmer of tears starting to well up in her beautiful eyes. How he wished she would say something, anything. Her silence tore at him worse than any words she might say, even in anger.

Feeling betrayed and defeated, Emma was determined to stay in control and not let Jake see her cry. Finally she said, "I want you out of my house."

"Em, you don't mean that?" Jake was starting to get frightened. He couldn't stand the thought that maybe he'd lost her.

"Yes, I do. I just can't be around you right now."

This time, Emma's words did not escape Jake's attention. She had said "right now." Maybe, in time, this would blow over and they could start again.

"Emma, please, I need to be able to protect you, to keep an eye on you."

"Isn't that what your cameras are for? So, you can watch me from the comfort of your cabin?" Her sarcasm pricked his conscience like a thousand needles.

"Things are getting too hot." She was aware that his comment held a double meaning. "I need to be closer to you than that."

Walking to the back door, she opened it for him. "Then you'll have to do it from the barn because I don't want you in my house tonight."

Stepping through the screen door onto the porch, he pleaded with her one more time. "Em, please?"

"No!"

Turning to go down the steps, he heard her parting shot. "And, just so you know, that number in my address book didn't belong to David, it belonged to Allison."

Jake glanced back over his shoulder, a puzzled expression on his face. "Allison?"

"Yes, Allison."

With that, Emma slammed the door shut. Jake remained on the porch, trying to come to grips with this new information. In the quiet, his ears picked up the sound of crying coming from the other side of the door. He felt like his heart was being ripped in two because he knew that the pain she was experiencing was all his fault. He promised himself that if it took the rest of his life, he would make it up to her.

Stepping off the porch, Jake felt the first raindrops start to fall. The night was black and lifeless, as the thunderclouds rumbled their way across the sky covering up any source of light from the heavens. Questions were racing through his mind as he processed what Emma had just told him. Could David have been pretending to be Allison in order to keep tabs on Emma? And, if that was true, then where was Allison? An uneasy feeling came over him, as he reflected back on the body that had been found in town. Jake thought of going back to the house, but, he was sure that Emma would be in no mood to listen right now. He would have to take shelter in the barn tonight, and try again in the morning.

"Hello, Jake." The voice that came out of the darkness from

behind him froze Jake in his tracks. He knew immediately who it belonged to and, because he did, he was also sure he must be hearing things. Easing his way back around, Jake searched the darkness to determine where the voice had come from. As his eyes adjusted to what little light there was, he saw a figure materialize out of the inky shadows of the house.

"You don't seem very glad to see me?" Death's icy fingers traced their way up Jake's spine. He was trying to bring into focus the misty silhouette in front of him, when the sky was split apart by a brilliant, flash of lightning. Jake felt his limbs become paralyzed, as he stared into the all too familiar face before him.

"Laura?!"

"That's right, Jake. It's me."

"It can't be. You're dead."

"Not quite."

Jake never heard the gun go off, as its sound was covered by another clap of thunder exploding in the sky. All he saw was a flash from the muzzle of a .38 special, then felt a powerful burning in his upper chest and shoulder as the bullet ripped through his flesh. The impact sent him sprawling backwards on the lawn. Lying there, staring into the black abyss above, the old woman's word popped into his mind—"This evil will have a face you know." Squinting to try to keep the rain out of his eyes, he could see Laura kneeling beside him. Jake felt her patting him down, finding both the gun in his shoulder holster and the one strapped to his ankle. He could hear the thud both of them made as she threw them out into the middle of the yard.

Brushing the hair back off of his face, Laura said, "The game's been fun, my sweet, but, time's running out, and so we'll have to end it."

"I don't understand." Jake voice sounded weak to his ears, and his breathing was harsh. "You were dead."

"That's what I wanted everyone to think. I've been devising a plan all along. You see, I knew that after the trial there would be no one there to protect me, and that Doug would never allow me to live after testifying against him."

"If you would've testified, he would've been in jail for the rest of his life."

"Maybe. But, he would've still made sure I was dead."

"Why? What would he have gained?"

"Oh, about five million dollars."

"What?!"

"You see, before I turned myself in, I managed to hide the biggest pay off Doug ever got. Even in jail, he would've had someone come after me. My child and I would've been looking behind us for the rest of our lives, unless he thought I was dead."

"But I saw your body." Jake was aware of a warm, stickiness running down his side, as he tried to remain conscious. He had to hang on a little longer because he needed to know what really happened that night.

"No, what you saw was my sister's body. Didn't know I had a twin sister, did you? That's why I had to cut off her hands because I knew our prints would be different. Anyway, she was my only living relative, and even though we weren't very close, I knew if something happened to me she would fight like hell to get custody of my child. After all, I did name my little girl after her."

Jake's mind raced through its memory banks as he tried to remember what Laura's little girl's name was. It was on the tip of his brain, which was becoming foggier by the minute. What was it? Sally? No, that wasn't quite right. Allie. That was it, Allie. But, had that been short for something? Allison? That's right, the baby's name had been Allison. It was then the awful truth hit him. He didn't want to believe it, but, the facts were there.

"Allison Black is your sister, isn't she?"

"Was. She was my sister. I simply traded lives with her. As Allison, I have everything. My child, a good reputation, a great job, and money. What more could a girl want?" Although Laura was bragging about her good fortune, Jake could still detect the bitterness in her voice.

"So, you planned to murder her that night."

"Actually, no. Things just happen to work out that way. I had contacted her a few days before, when you thought I called Allie's doctor. I was trying to figure out when and where to do it, when she happen to come by while you were out. I just figured why not take advantage of the situation."

Jake was feeling sick to his stomach. He couldn't hear the slightest sound of remorse in Laura's voice for what she'd done. She talked about the whole thing as if it were just another step in some sort of business plan she had developed.

"Jake, I know you must be lying there thinking that I'm some kind of cold-hearted bitch, but, you know, Allison really didn't know how to live life to the fullest, not like I did. I like to think she gave her life for a better cause."

"You really are sick." Jake couldn't hide the disgust he felt for her. "All the time that I was protecting you, I thought about how much you deserved a new start. You'll never know what it did to me to come back and find you dead. It took me years to come to grips with it. And, now, I find out it wasn't even you."

"You know, Jake, I really loved you, even though you only used me. First, you slept with me, and then told me that it had been a mistake. You know, we could've been great together, but, you were never going to give it a chance. I guess knowing what I was going to put you through was just icing on the cake for me."

Jake knew she was right, he had used her. He had made a grave mistake by getting personally involved with a witness. It had only been the day before her supposed death that Jake had broken it off. He'd finally admitted to himself it was lust, not love, and that their affair could destroy his career. Fortunately, no one had ever found out about it. Jake closed his eyes as a wave of pain shot through him. He was losing blood, and he could feel himself slipping toward oblivion. However, there was one more question he needed an answer to.

"I understand your hatred for me, but, why are you after Emma?"

"You know, I do wish I didn't have to kill her, but, somewhere in the back of her mind, she knows I killed Charles."

Jake could feel a black void over taking him, swallowing him whole. From what seemed like a great distance he could hear Laura's voice.

"I'll be back to see you later. But, for now, Jake darlin', I need to pay a visit to Emma."

# Chapter Twenty-Five

The sense of betrayal was so overwhelming that Emma couldn't hold back her tears. Angrily, she wiped them from her flushed cheeks, and wondered why she ever trusted him. How had she let her head be turned so easily by a handsome face? Feeling humiliated and embarrassed, Emma realized just how much of her life Jake must have seen and heard before she even knew he existed. Her suspicions of being watched in her own home had not been her imagination after all. Hidden underneath her current hurt, she knew he had been trying to protect her the best way he knew how, but, she still felt her trust had been violated. Even now, the thought of the cameras being in the house, and not knowing where they were, made her uncomfortable. The anger inside of her was mixed with feelings of loss and sadness, and the thought of giving up the possible love she had just found brought an unbelievable ache to her soul. Maybe a glass of wine and a hot bath would help her relax. Reaching for the handle on the refrigerator, she flashed back to last night's romantic encounter, and her eyes started to once again fill with tears. Turning out the kitchen light, she decided instead to go straight to bed. The incessant noise from the storm outside almost caused her to miss the knock at the front door.

"I wonder what other surprises he needs to tell me about," Emma muttered to herself.

Undoing the dead bolt, Emma opened the door bent upon sending Jake back to the barn. Her face lit up, however, when she found her friend standing on the porch.

"Allison! My, God, what are you doing here?"

"Can't I just come and see how my best friend's doing?"

"Of course you can. Please come in."

Allison stepped into the living room, leaving behind a trail of water that was dripping off her clothes.

"Good, Lord," Emma said, "It must be really pouring out there. You got soaked just running from your car to the door."

"Yeah, it's pretty nasty out."

"Let me get you a towel."

A deep growl brought Emma's attention back around towards the kitchen. Otis, who had been sitting under the kitchen table in a blue funk ever since she had exiled Jake from the house, was now standing in the doorway. His ears were flat against his head and the fur on his neck and back stood on end. A snarl was wrinkling up his nose, and little glimpses of white showed as he started to bare his teeth. Otis' eyes, those unnerving blue eyes, never once wavered as he zeroed in on Allison. Shocked at his behavior, Emma hurried over to the dog.

"Otis, what in the world is wrong with you." Emma's voice was hushed, but, stern. "You know Allison."

Otis never moved a muscle. The low grumble continued to rise up from his broad chest. Remembering that the dog had never been overly fond of Allison, Emma was still taken by surprise by Otis' hostile reaction.

Apologizing to Allison, Emma said, "I don't know what's

wrong with him. It's been one of those nights, you know. I'll put him outside. Come on, Otis." She walked past Otis towards the back door, expecting him to follow.

The dog ignored her, giving no indication that he had even heard her.

"Otis! Get over here." It was quite obvious that all of the dog's attention had become locked on his quarry in the living room.

Grabbing him by the collar, it took all the strength Emma could muster to drag him to the back door. Her only saving grace was the linoleum in the kitchen, which provided the dog with little traction, and allowed Emma to sort of slide him along the floor. She had never had to drag Otis anywhere before, and was surprised by the amount of strength the dog possessed. Holding him with one hand, she managed to open the door with the other. Half pulling, half shoving she was able to get Otis out onto the porch.

"I don't know what's gotten into you, but you can just join your friend in the barn." Emma said in a harsh whisper. "I don't have the strength to deal with either of you tonight."

For the first time since Allison's arrival, the big retriever turned his attention to Emma. He whimpered as he looked at her, and then back into the house. Softly taking her hand in his mouth, he tried to lead her off the porch steps.

Drawing her hand back, Emma scolded him, "Stop that! I'm not going with you. You just go on out to the barn right now." Appearing frightened, the dog whined and leaned up against her. Reaching down, she reassuringly stroked the sides of his face. "It's all right. It's just Allison." Kissing the top of his head, she said, "I'll see you in the morning."

Stepping back inside the house, Emma felt bad about having to put Otis outside on such a miserable night. If Allison didn't stay over, she would call him back inside before going to bed. Emma shook her head, still unable to figure out why the dog had reacted so. If Emma hadn't already been drained from her confrontation with Jake, she might have remembered what Martha Quinn had told her about the dog—"He's your guardian…In what is to come, you may doubt yourself, but do not doubt him." Tired and worn out, Emma returned to her guest in the living room, almost wishing that Allison had not shown up tonight. However, Emma hadn't seen her in months, and maybe a friendly visit was what she needed.

"I'm really sorry, Allison, I don't know what got into him. He's usually really well behaved."

"Oh, he probably just didn't recognize me. It has been a while, you know."

"I know. I also noticed that you're not a blonde anymore." Emma teased.

"I thought I'd try my real color for a change. You know, it's not really true that blondes have more fun." Allison's comment should have been taken as a joke, but there was nothing in her voice that suggested she meant it to be one.

Walking around the living room, Allison seemed to be taking stock of everything that was there. Stopping at the old roll top desk, she picked up the picture of herself and Emma that had been taken at one of the company picnics. Allison seemed to drift off, as she stared at the picture for several minutes.

"We were such good friends." Allison's words sounded wooden.

"What do you mean 'were'? We are good friends." Emma noticed the strange, vacant look in Allison's eyes. She was becoming quite concerned for her friend. "Allison, is everything okay?"

"It will be, after tonight."

Every nerve in Emma's body started to tingle. There was

something dreadfully wrong, and she was beginning to regret the fact that she had put Otis outside.

"Allison, why are you here?"

"I followed David down here."

"David?!" Emma's heart skipped a beat. Jake had been right after all. "What was David doing here?"

"Coming to see you. To talk to you about Charles."

"What about Charles?"

"I overheard him say he knew who killed him. Said that he had to get to you, had to tell you in person because you would never believe him over the phone." Allison refocused her gaze on Emma. "But, then, you already know who killed Charles."

"What are you talking about? I don't know who killed Charles."

"Yes, you do."

"No, I don't!" Emma's head started to hurt, and she was becoming very irritated with her friend.

"You do, and if you think about it long enough it'll come to you."

For what seemed like an eternity, the two of them just stared at each other, neither one uttering a word. A draft from a partially opened window carried a familiar scent to Emma that sent her brain racing back to the night of Charles' death. Where her dreams had always been surrounded in a mist, her waking memories were much more clear. She was walking through the bedroom, and every detail was now sharp. The coals in the fireplace looked like red, hot lava under a darkened layer of volcanic crust. She could see the bright, orange button that was lit on the phone, and she could hear the buzzing coming from the receiver lying on the floor. The scene before her on the bed was tragic, but, she couldn't help noticing just how vibrant the color of the blood was on the sheets. A sweet aroma enticed her to look up into the mirror, and this time the features of the face were sharp and distinct. Emma knew there was no question as to whom those cornflower blue eyes belonged. She also now knew what the fragrance was she had been smelling—a perfume—Allison's perfume.

Emma couldn't keep the pain out of her eyes as she spoke, "You killed Charles."

"Yes, I did. And, David, too."

"David? Why David?"

"If he really had figured it all out, I couldn't let him live."

A loud crack of thunder shook the house, reminding Emma of the storm raging outside. As the terror starting rising inside her, she couldn't help but think that the night was quite fitting for what was now transpiring. Not only was she again wishing that she hadn't put Otis outside, but, was very much regretting that she had banished Jake to the barn. Emma looked at the door, hoping against hope that he had seen Allison's car, and would come to investigate.

"If you're waiting for Jake to rescue you, I'm afraid you're going to have a long wait." Allison said, "He's feeling a little under the weather right now."

Emma was unable to hide the fear that was keeping her from asking the obvious question, terrified of what the answer would be. Reading her mind, Allison continued, "He was still alive when I left him. But, you know, I sure wouldn't want to be out there on a night like this."

# Chapter Twenty-Six

In his dream, Jake was drowning. The water was dark and murky. Every time he tried to get a breath he choked on the acrid water that filled his mouth. The pain in his arm kept hindering Jake's efforts as he struggled to swim towards the dim light overhead. An angelic face, with eyes the color of the sea, beckoned to him from above, only to dissipate into the waves whenever he reached for it. Jake knew there was somewhere he desperately needed to be, but, the only thing he could concentrate on right now was breathing. He couldn't die, not like this. From the shadows below, bony fingers climbed their way upwards, trying to draw him down into their depths. Just as the last of Jake's strength began to wain, he felt his body, by no power of his own, start rising to the surface. Breaking free of the watery grave, he took in a deep breath of sweet air.

The icy sting of the rain on his face brought Jake out of his dream world. He could feel himself being dragged through the puddles and mud, that were forming in the water soaked grass. Starting to panic, he was sure Laura must have returned to finish what she started, and that he was now too late to save Emma. A warm breath on his ear and a cold nose against the back of neck told him, however, that his savior had arrived. The dog had a firm grip on the back of his shirt, and was, unceremoniously, pulling him toward the safety of the barn. It only took a few minutes, but it felt like hours, before Jake could no longer feel the rain battering his body. He had become chilled to the bone, and though he was no longer out in the freezing rain and wind, the barn wasn't much warmer. Otis had pulled him into the first stall inside the barn, and Jake covered himself with a layer straw in an attempt to reserve what little body heat he had left. From out of the dark, he felt Otis' soft tongue lick his cheek, causing him to jump.

"Guess I owe you one, big guy. I don't know why she put you outside tonight, but, I'm sure glad she did." Reaching out he buried his hand in the retriever's wet coat. "I still need your help though. We've got to get back to the house."

Using the dog for support, Jake started to rise up on his good arm, only to succumb to a wave of dizziness that caused him to fall back into the hay. Warm blood still oozed from his shoulder. He knew he needed to do something to stop it, but, he was tired, very tired. Otis, who had been padding around him in a circle, curled up next to him. Whether the dog really knew what he was doing, or it was just dumb luck, Otis had managed to place himself right up against Jake's open wound, stifling the flow of blood. The last thing Jake remembered before closing his eyes, was the welcoming warmth from the big dog's body as it started to penetrate his own.

\* \* \*

Emma could no longer hold back the question she wanted to ask Allison.

"How do you know Jake?"

Allison, whose face had been unreadable most of the night, appeared to be taken back by Emma's question.

"You surprise me, Emma. I come all the way here to tell you I killed Charles, and your biggest concern is how I know Jake? I figured you would ask that sooner or later, but not this early in our conversation."

"Are you going to answer my question?"

"Let's just say I know him from a long time ago. Before I even met you."

"From where?"

Taunting her, Allison said, "I think I'll save that for later. Don't you want to know about Charles? Aren't you at least a little bit curious about why I killed him?"

"I suppose I should be, but, I'm not sure I care anymore."

"Remember when you told me that you suspected Charles of having an affair." Emma nodded. "Well, he was. With me."

The hurt was plain on Emma's face. "But, you were my best friend."

"Ah, yes, but all's fair in love and war as they say."

"Charles loved you?"

"Is that so hard to believe?" Allison said defensively. "You think you were the only one Charles could ever love."

"No. I just didn't think he was capable of loving anyone, that's all."

"Charles would have married me if it hadn't been for you."

Emma knew that Allison was not only lying to her, but to herself. As his secretary, Charles had always treated Allison as a second-class citizen, and had spoken even worse of her behind her back. Emma, however, had no doubt that Charles had had an affair with Allison because, simply put, Charles would have used any woman who was willing to let him. It was becoming obvious now that Allison had been more than willing.

"Allison, Charles never loved you, we both know that. Besides, if you were so sure he loved you, why didn't you kill me instead? Then he would've been free to marry you."

The tortured look on Allison's face told Emma she had hit a nerve. Allison's voice was full of venom as she spoke. "I went to him that night to tell him that I was pregnant."

"Pregnant?!"

"It turned out I wasn't, but, I thought I was when I went to him. We'd been seeing each other for over 6 months, and I was sure he'd leave you once he knew. But do you know what he told me?" Emma shook her head, even though she was pretty sure what Charles' answer had been. As Allison continued, Emma was proven right. "He told me to get an abortion. An abortion! And, if I didn't he said he would deny everything. I told him that I would force him into a paternity test, and he said that no matter how the test came back that he would never leave you. He said he'd never marry me because I would never fit in with his friends. The bastard called me a two bit whore, and said he could make me miserable for the rest of my life. On top of it all, he fired me. Said he never wanted to see me again. I made certain he would never see anything again."

The image of Charles' eyeless face flashed in Emma's mind. It was hard for her to imagine that Allison could've done something so monstrous. She'd never been afraid of anyone in her life more than she was of Allison at this moment. However, as strange as it might seem, a small part of Emma was able to at least comprehend what had happened. After all, she'd been married to Charles, and knew what kind of a selfish, uncaring individual he could be. He had a way of driving people beyond their limits, and she had always known it was just a matter of time before he would push someone too far. Unfortunately, that someone had turned out to be Allison. But, Emma also knew that Allison was insane.

She'd already admitted to killing David, she'd left Jake for dead, and now she was here to kill her. Seeing no other option at this time, Emma's only hope was to keep her talking.

"Why did you take Charles' wedding ring? It was the only thing missing."

Pulling a necklace out from under her sweater, Emma cringed when she realized it was Charles' ring hanging around Allison's neck.

"I guess I just wanted a memento, and he didn't seem to need it anymore."

"You know, if the police had continued their investigation, they would've caught you."

"I know. That's why I convinced Aaron that their continued investigation could cause a lot of damage to the firm. He must have taken what I said to heart because he went downtown and pulled some strings."

"What makes you think that they won't catch you for David's murder, or Jake's, or mine?"

"Because after tonight, I won't be in the country. Allie's waiting for me at my aunt's in Kansas City, and then we're flying out of here."

"And, just how will you live?"

"Oh, I have prospects."

"Allison, you need help. If you turn yourself in, I'll see to it that you get that help. I promise."

Allison's laugh bordered on hysteria. "You promise to help me? How big a fool do you think I am? We both know that they'll lock me up for the rest of my life, if they don't fry me first. Sorry, Emma, but it's over, and I need to be getting on my way."

Emma had never felt as helpless as she did now. While watching Allison pull a gun out from underneath her sweater, everything seem to shift into slow motion. Even their voices sounded like a record being played at the wrong speed.

"Allison, don't do this."

"This is the way it has to be, Emma."

The sound of breaking glass and splitting wood echoed from the kitchen, diverting Allison's attention. Taking the small opportunity afforded her, Emma grabbed for the gun, struggling to wrench it from Allison's grasp. Allison was a big boned woman, with a definite advantage in both height and weight, so it didn't take long before Emma found herself sliding across the hardwood floor, slamming into the wood burning stove. She heard her ribs crack, as the breath was knocked out of her. Looking up, she found herself staring one more time down the barrel of Allison's gun.

"Laura!" Jake's voice boomed from the kitchen doorway. "Put the gun down."

"Laura?" Emma gave Allison a puzzling look.

"Laura, do you hear me? Put the gun down."

"Allison, is he talking to you?"

Complete panic and confusion filled Allison's face. She was becoming very disoriented, as she tried to figure out where the biggest threat to her was coming from. The rage that had been building in her for days was about to release itself. Swinging the gun away from Emma, she faced Jake, who had moved into the living room.

"Give me the gun, Laura. You don't want to do this. Think about Allie." Jake words were soft, and he edged his way towards her.

"You don't understand, Jake. This is the only way out for me."

"No, it isn't. I'll help you, I promise."

Eyeing him maniacally, she said, "What's with you two? Did you rehearse this, or something? You both want to help me?"

Jake's steps faltered, and he grimaced in pain.

Giving him a look of pity, she said, "You can't even help yourself, Jake."

The sound of distant sirens was becoming audible through the noise of the storm.

"Listen to that, Laura." Jake said through gritted teeth. "They'll be here soon. You won't be able to get away this time."

"You may be right, Jake, but at least I will have finished what I came here to do."

With that, Allison pulled the trigger. For the second time that night, Jake felt his body torn apart by a bullet, as this one entered his side. Screaming in agony, he fell to the floor. He heard Emma yell out his name, and saw Allison bring the gun back around in her direction. He knew that nothing less than a miracle could save them now.

The deranged woman standing before Emma was not the friend she had known. Not knowing who she was, Emma was at a loss for words. Jake had called her Laura. It was obvious they'd crossed paths somewhere in the past. Emma glanced over at Jake's body, and noticed he appeared to still be breathing, although his blood was quickly spreading in a pool over the hardwood floor. The sirens were growing louder, and Emma could only pray that they would get there before Allison tried to finish what she had set out to do.

"Why did he call you Laura?" Emma asked, stalling for time.

"Because that's my name."

"No, it's not. It's Allison."

"No, it's Laura. Allison is my sister."

"Your sister?" Emma asked cautiously.

"That's right. She works for some big law firm in Denver."

"I know. Allison, why don't you give me the gun."

"My name's not Allison." Angry and confused, she centered the gun at Emma chest.

Holding her breath, Emma's eyes remained transfixed on the gun. Allison's hand was steady as she started to apply pressure to the trigger. From out of nowhere, a black blur streaked across the room, hitting Allison in the back just as the gun went off. Emma heard the bullet whiz by her ear and ricochet off the cast iron stove. Otis was now standing his ground between Emma and Allison. The low, menacing growl coming from his throat was more threatening than any ferocious barking, or snarling could have been. Managing to regain her footing, Allison now pointed the gun at the dog.

"Otis!" Emma screamed, "Get out of the way! Run!"

The dog turned and ran towards the couch on the other side of the room, drawing the fire away from Emma. As the gun discharged, Emma heard a yelp as Otis disappeared behind the large sofa. Enough was enough. Grabbing the closest thing she could find, Emma let out a rebel yell that could have raised the dead. Alarmed, Allison spun back around, lunging in Emma's direction. She never saw the fireplace poker that Emma had stretched out before her. Horrified, Emma looked on as Allison impaled herself on the point of the cast iron rod. Dropping the gun, Allison grabbed the protruding end of the poker with both hands. Tilting her head to one side, she looked at Emma with a curious expression on her face. A sudden spark of recognition filled her eyes, and for the first time since this evening's nightmare had begun, Allison seemed to realize the consequences of all she'd done. Sliding to the floor, she reached out for Emma, a look of sorrow and regret on her face. She would die remembering what she and Emma once had. Staring at the lifeless form before her, Emma was uncertain of what she was supposed to feel.

From across the room, she heard Jake's groan. Rushing to his side, Emma knelt down and cradled his head in her arms. Taking off her shirt, she wadded it up, pressing it against the new wound in his side. A strange scratching noise startled her. Looking around, she spotted Otis crawling across the floor toward her.

Reaching her, he laid his head up on her thigh. She could see the blood from where the bullet had hit him on his right flank. Her eyes started to fill up with tears. Her heros. They had saved her life, and she'd be damned if she was going to let either of them die.

A weak moan escaped Jake's lips, and he opened his eyes. Relief flooded through him, when he saw Emma's face. He was certain since he was in her arms that Laura must be dead. Jake tried to lift his hand to her face, but the pain was too great. She grabbed his hand, squeezing it tightly.

"Don't die on me, Jake. Help's almost here, so don't die on me now." Her voice cracked with emotion. She was trying hard to fight back the tears that wanted to cascade from her eyes.

It hurt like hell for him to talk, but, he had to reassure her. "I'm not going anywhere."

Neither of them seem to notice the sound of sirens coming from the yard, or that the room was now filled with a rainbow of colors from the red, blue, and yellow strobe lights peeking their way in through window shades. They could only stare into each other's eyes, looking for the future they both hoped to find there.

Taking another haggard breath, Jake smiled his crooked smile. "I love you, Em."

Her tears overflowed, leaving a delicate trail down her cheeks. "I love you, too, Jake, with all my heart."

# Epilogue

Emma relaxed on the large porch of her log home that was nestled high in the Rockies just outside of Grand Lake, Colorado. Early morning rays of sunshine broke over the top of the mountains, warming her face. The fresh scent of pine drifted to her on the crisp autumn air, causing her to pull the green and lavender comforter up closer around her shoulders. The comforter had shown up in the mail a few days prior to their wedding day, postmarked Cedar Falls, Missouri. The comforter and the old rocker, in which she now sat, were the only keepsakes of the Ozarks that Emma had. Sipping on her coffee, she looked out across the beautiful valley with it's sparkling, clear stream which was fed by the snow pack from the peaks that surrounded it. The upper slopes of the mountains were starting to change color, and the aspen leaves shimmered like golden coins in the sun.

Sounds of happy barking brought her attention back around to the barn and corrals that lay south of the house. A warm, peaceful feeling flooded through her as she watched the scene taking place before her. Jake was busy trying to feed their horses, a task made much more difficult by Otis' insistence that Jake play with him. Jake was scolding him for being underfoot, and as usual the dog paid him little mind. The two of them had become inseparable since that night almost a year ago, and Emma was grateful to the intervening powers above that they'd all survived.

Jake had spent almost a month in the hospital recuperating, with Emma at his side every day. Otis healed faster and, due to his hero status, had been allowed to visit Jake, all the while charming every nurse who saw him. The remnants of the storm that Allison created in her life, had left Emma feeling unsettled, and with the need to start over, again. Within the first week of putting the old farmhouse on the market, it sold—furniture and all. She and Otis had moved into the little cabin Jake had been renting until he was released from the hospital. However, one good thing had come out of all the chaos, and that was the absence of her old nightmares. Since that night, Emma had been able to sleep, unhindered by past horrors.

Matt had also survived, thanks to Maggie, but, a slight limp would always be a reminder to him of what happened. Out of their ordeal, the four of them had forged a close friendship, standing up for each other at their respective weddings. Jake and Emma's had been a small ceremony, right here on the porch of their new home, with Otis being the ring bearer. Lieutenant Roger Harris, and his new girlfriend, Katherine, had been in attendance, with Harris graciously stepping in to give Emma away. Matt and Maggie, however, had surprised everyone by heading to Las Vegas, taking with them only Jake, Emma, and, of course, Otis. Thanksgiving was now less than a month away, and Emma was looking forward to seeing their friends who would be spending it with them, including Henry, who, unfortunately, had been unable to come to their wedding.

Having finished the morning chores, Jake waved at her, flashing her one of his gorgeous smiles, as he and Otis headed back for the house. Emma's heart swelled with love and pride for them, and she was so happy that her wish upon that evening star had been granted. A cool breeze tickled the little curls on the back of her neck, and she snuggled deeper into her quilt, thinking of the only words Martha Quinn had written on the note that had accompanied the comforter—"Always trust in your heart."